POTTERVILLE MIDDLE SCHOOL

Left Hand Wood

ILLUSTRATED BY NIGEL LAMBOURNE
COVER PAINTING BY LEWIS PARKER

Left Hand Wood

George Furnell

F FOLLETT PUBLISHING COMPANY
CHICAGO

CONTENTS

1 An April the First   11

2 A Bramble Bath   21

3 Roger Alone   30

4 The Bristolites   41

5 Roger Again   46

6 Pine Tree Quarry Picnic   57

7 Alb 'Erratt   68

8 Meetings and Farewells   79

9 Seven Long Weeks   87

10 Left Hand Wood   96

11 Middle Finger and Wrist   107

12 The Secret Shared   126

13 The Dragon's Cave   137

14 Ferns, Barrs, and Burrows   150

15 The Holes   173

16 No Other Way   184

17 The Fifth Hole   203

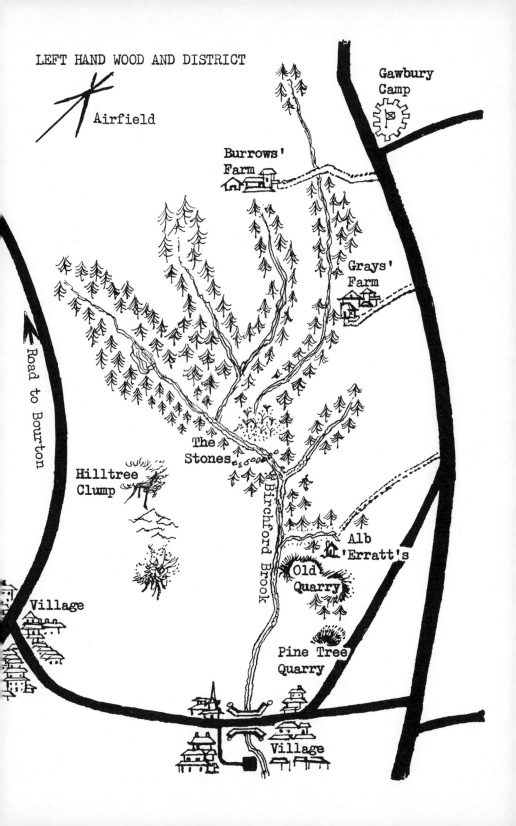

Left Hand Wood

1
An April the First

Roger Fern, sitting in the bottom of Tim's toy-cupboard, was beginning to feel acutely uncomfortable and slightly silly. He wondered how much longer he could stand it. His knees were jammed up against his cheeks. The shelf of the cupboard was so low that his head was forced down. His feet only fitted in if he splayed them out ridiculously widely, and his left ankle with the big football bruise on it was already aching foully. Underneath his bent-up legs, a most awkward cushion, was his father's tape recorder, with the power wires trailing about somewhere, and a pocket flashlight just within fingertip grasp. Roger's hands, if he forced them, could just bend in the correct dislocated angles to work the switches of the recorder, and the flashlight was small enough to be held in his mouth (and luckily too big to swallow) for when the time came to shut the cupboard door and begin the trick. But why didn't they come? Why didn't they come before he stifled, got a cramp or some joint cracked up and crippled him for life?

"They" were his cousins from Bristol, the "Bristolites" as Roger, now nearly twelve years old, Stephen his older brother, and Tim, aged five, had always called them. The Bristolites, the five Barr children with their mother and father, were due to arrive at about twelve on a short visit, and Roger was determined to give them the surprise of their lives when they arrived . . . if they ever did. That was why he was compressed into the hurriedly emptied toy-cupboard, on the top of which the telephone sat, and why Tim, with an old telescope, was peering out of a bedroom window, keeping a lookout up the road for the black Humber car of the Bristolites, and why Stephen and Mr. and Mrs. Fern were, on Roger's strict orders, waiting, ready to rush upstairs to hide under the bed.

"It's them, I think," yelled Tim suddenly. "This te'scope's gone all cloudy, but I think, I think . . ."

"Oh, lord!" groaned Roger. He yelled, "Steve, go and look, quick!" What a time for doubts! Then he felt his muscles tighten, his breathing quicken, as Stephen called down the staircase, "Yes, it is them, Rog. They're coming up the path. Good luck! Come on, Mum and Dad!"

Roger saw his father and mother scurry past and heard

them hurrying up the stairs as he pulled the cupboard door tight shut. He fumbled for the flashlight, switched it on, and put it in his mouth. Below him the green eye of the tape recorder glowed eerily. His fingers tightened on the starting switch. He heard voices at the door of the cottage and chuckled in excitement. The light was making him dribble. Saliva was dripping down his chin. He heard the door open. A few seconds of silence, then a voice called, "Anybody home?"

Auntie, thought Roger. Wait for it . . . wait for it. Puzzled sounds multiplied.

"Where are they all?"

"No one in that room."

"Have a look round the back."

Roger could wait no longer. He let go of the release knob, the recorder spools began whirring softly—and the telephone rang.

Mr. Fern, wriggling on his face under the bed, grinned at Mrs. Fern a few inches away. "Roger hasn't stifled yet then," he breathed.

"Sshh . . . listen!"

They heard Tim tittering loudly under the bed in the next room until a loud hiss from Stephen quieted him.

The telephone kept ringing.

"Answer it, Daddy," came a voice from the living room.

"It might be Auntie or Unk ringing up to tell us they'll be late back from shopping in Cambridge or something."

("That's Mary, isn't it?" hissed Mr. Fern. "Or Anne.")

"Answer it and see, Daddy."

"Yes, I will," came Dr. Barr's voice. He sounded puzzled as he picked up the telephone.

The telephone stopped ringing.

"Hello? That's funny—no one there."

The listeners heard the instrument rattle on its rest. *Brring-brring; brring-brring*, it began, and was picked up again.

"Hello? Funny—only the buzzing. Hello? Hey, there's still just the buzzing—listen."

"It's out of order. Oh, I know, they've forgotten to press Button A."

"Hello—is anyone there? Have you pressed Button A?" Silence.

"This is daft. There's no one there." The telephone was put down.

Brring-brring-brring-brring.

"Oh no!" Dr. Barr sounded exasperated, "Hello! Hello! There's no one there. What's the matter with the thing!" The "thing" was almost slammed down this time. It began again immediately. *Brring-brring, brring-brring.*

Mr. Fern, his chin a little sore from being wriggled on a bedroom carpet, was by now highly amused. He was chuckling so much that Mrs. Fern felt sure he would be heard by the puzzled Bristolites below. "Good old Roger!" he gasped. "He's got 'em puzzled!"

Then feet sounded on the stairs. Mrs. Barr's voice

said, "I'll have a look upstairs." One of the children ran up after her.

They're bound to find Stephen and Tim, thought Mr. Fern. Tim will never keep still or quiet.

But the steps, after halting in the doorways of the two other bedrooms, started again along the little landing and came into the room where Mr. and Mrs. Fern were lying under the bed, now feeling a little foolish at the thought of being found there. But they were not found. Their sister-in-law's legs stopped a few yards inside the room. They saw her feet turn and heard her say, "No one here either, Jane." Then Mr. Fern, restraining himself from reaching out to grab a foot, heard the two baffled seekers going down the stairs.

Brring-brring, brring-b—!

As the mysterious telephone ringing started again, the puzzled comments of the seven Bristolites could again be heard from below. Luckily, the noise of the ringing bell and the chatter of five children and their parents covered the loud chuckling from Stephen and Tim in one room and Mr. and Mrs. Fern in the other. Dr. Barr still could not understand how a telephone could act so oddly. He was beginning to snap.

"Hello? No—just buzzing again. That's all." He put it down. It rang immediately again. *Brring.* He snatched it up. The ringing stopped. He put it down. The ringing started. "It's mad!" He picked it up again, and said, "I'm going to report this." He dialed and then spoke. "Hello, exchange? I want to report a fault. This phone keeps ringing and yet . . ."

A loud yell of alarm suddenly came from behind him. The Bristolite girls were suddenly shouting, "There's Roger!"

"Ooh, you did scare me!"

"Gosh, when that cupboard started opening! It was the tape recorder!"

Dr. Barr stood startled, with the telephone in his hand; then, absently, he said, "Thank you, exchange. It's all right now," and was deafened by a triumphant Roger bellowing, "April Fools! April Fools!"

Twice during the meal that followed the hilarious reunion of the two families, Uncle Donald had suddenly grinned hugely to himself and burst out laughing.

"Roger, you young varmint! Proper April Fools you made us all! Well done, the Ferns!"

And that had started the giggling and the explanations and the laughing memories again.

"Don't you ever look under beds, Doris?"

"Ooh, it was spooky when the toy-cupboard door started opening!"

"I thought I should burst when someone kept saying, 'Have you pressed Button A?'"

"I wanted to grab your foot, Jane. It was only about an inch from my nose—"

"I kept lookout with the telescope, Uncle."

"I felt a bit of a fool, lying under the bed, but George was just like one of the kids, giggling to himself."

"Oooh, it was funny. You kept saying, 'Have you pressed Button A?'"

"Whose idea was it to record the phone ringing?"

"It sounded exactly like the phone."

"Well, it was only a few inches underneath, wasn't it?"

"Did you press the button and get the fourpence back, Steve?"

"What fourpence, Rog?"

"When he went along to the village phone-box and rang this number, so I could record the ringing."

"Oh, yes."

"Jolly good, Rog. Best April Fools' joke I've heard of for a long time."

"You wait till you come to Bristol, Auntie Norah!"

"We'll have an August Fools' Day, won't we, Pete?"

And so it went on, until even the youngest ones had a faint notion of how the trick had been played. Tim wanted to go there and then, in the middle of the ice cream and bananas, to be shown how you pressed Button A in the telephone-box. For the rest of the day he kept muttering happily to himself, like a wizard chanting a spell, "Have you pressed Button A? Have you pressed the button, eh? Have you—?" and asking everyone who came near him, "Is it August Fools' Day tomorrow?"

April Fools' Day had been on a Saturday. The seven Barrs had stayed with the Ferns over the weekend and then returned to Bristol, but not before the next meeting had been arranged, for they were all an affectionate family and the children were not old enough to find the gathering of the clan anything but good fun. They had all met, on various Whitsunday and August holidays in the past, at a favorite spot of theirs for a picnic, a really grand affair with a full-scale feast, always including yards and yards of sausages cooked over a big wood fire. There were games of cricket, French cricket, hide-and-seek and un-limited wandering over wide miles of glorious Cots-wold fields and woods.

The spot they had found was more or less halfway between the Barrs in Bristol and the Ferns near Cam-bridge. It was a tiny, long disused and forgotten quarry, where once fine Cotswold stone had been dug up, but which now for three hundred and sixty-three days a year saw only rabbits and blackbirds and other creatures of the wild. On the other two days it echoed to the shouts of the twelve Barrs and Ferns, the crackle of their fires and the sizzling of their sausages—and occasionally their moans about the washing up. Where stones had once been plundered, nature had covered the scars with fine turf and a profusion of wild flowers. The diggings had never been very deep and now the edges, high enough to be exciting but not so steep as to be dangerous, were clothed and softened with bushes of hawthorn and sloe and young birch trees. Between the quarry and the road was a group of superb pine trees for a landmark, giving a name to the place.

This was where Mrs. Fern had suggested a meeting on Easter Monday, just a week after the Barrs went home. Everyone had agreed eagerly. They had never been at Easter before, but the weather seemed settled, and football could be played just as well as any other game there in the meadow beyond the quarry. And if it was a bit colder at

Easter than at Whitsunday, why not take twice as many sausages? . . . Easy!

Roger and Stephen Fern had decided on another innovation this time too. They had both agreed that no self-respecting Barr could possibly let the April Fools' telephone joke go unrevenged, and that this forthcoming meeting at Pine Tree Quarry was the obvious time for some counterattack to be planned by the very brainy Jane and Sarah, with, no doubt, plenty of willing help from young Mary and the twins Anne and Peter. It was clear that to arrive at the picnic in the car, as usual, would be to ask for it, to walk straight into danger. The Bristolites could get there earlier if they wanted to and set up traps.

"What, those huge things with metal teeth that snap shut when you tread on 'em and bite you in two?" said Roger.

"No, you idiot," grinned Stephen, "something like nooses of rope in the grass to trip us up, or bushes that wham you in the face . . . Oh, you know." Little Tim, hearing this, hoped that he would be brave if the Bristolites did catch him in some awful trap.

The upshot was that, after looking at their father's map of the picnic district, the boys decided to send their bicycles on by train to a station ten miles short of their destination. On the day of the picnic they would go in the car with their parents and Tim as far as the station, collect their cycles, and ride the rest of the way, arriving "round the back somewhere"—as Roger put it—"so we can see what the girls are up to. " The land around the rendezvous was delightful up-and-down country. The thought of cycling

added to the thrill of the day they were looking forward
to so much

So it was on Easter Monday at about eleven o'clock
on a bright-periods-and-possibly-light-showers sort of
morning Roger and Stephen collected their cycles from
the tiny Left Luggage office at Dingham station. They
waved good-bye to Tim and their mother and father,
started off down the road southwest toward the picnic,
turned around after twenty yards and raced back to get
the map they had forgotten to take out of the car, and
then set off to thwart whatever fiendish plans their cousins
had made for them at Pine Tree Quarry.

2
A Bramble Bath

After half an hour's riding, Stephen and Roger got a
little stiffly off their bicycles and leaned them against the
gateway. They had ridden five miles and had both begun
to feel like a breather. On each side of the field gate there
was a thick hedge of hawthorn and brambles, which
looked as if it had not been cut for years. Almost hidden
by the thick, high hedge stood a post, just inside the field.
The post had once been painted, but the paint had worn
off until now only the faintest traces of white were left,
and the grain of the wood showed through. On top of
the post was a green notice-board. Here too the lettering
had worn and paled.

Roger, always curious, scrambled up the gate to the top-most bar and called out, "Hey, Steve, there's a notice-board here. Come and look." Stephen looked over the rickety gate. Roger was reading out, "B-u-r-y . . . Some-thing-bury Camp. P-r-e-h, prehistoric earthworm."

"Earthwork, idiot," scoffed Stephen. "I can't see any earthworks, only those airfield hangars miles away over there. See them? And a plane just landing?"

"Dunno—I can't see much at all. Too many brambles all around the post." Roger stepped up onto the last bar of the gate, reaching over to the post and notice-board. Stephen gave a warning yell. "Careful! That gate's a bit weak, Rog!"

" 'S O.K. Roger gasped, as he struggled to keep his balance, to hold on to the notice-board post, and to keep the brambles clear of his face. "These briars are jolly sharp—yow!" He gave a piercing yell as a briar he had been holding back from the post slipped out of his fingers. The bramble slashed wickedly across him, the thorns scratching grooves across his cheeks.

Stephen, watching, saw the scratches go white, then immediately redden as blood began oozing out. He called out again. "Be careful, Rog! Don't go and get one of them in your eyes. Let me come and see: I'm a bit taller than you." He began climbing up the gate.

Roger snapped immediately, "No! Don't! You silly fool, Steve. I can reach. Don't jerk the gate! You'll have me off! Ow!" He gave a howl as the top bar of the old gate wobbled, cracked loose from the upright, and broke.

Stephen saw a foot kick backward and felt it crash into his eye. He fell off the gate and rolled onto the grass. His eye and cheek hurt so much that he hardly noticed the agonized squeal Roger gave as he too fell, forward, into the middle of the bramble bush.

"You stupid, clumsy fool!" Stephen growled, getting up off the grass and rubbing his eye. He clambered over the broken bars of the old gate and then stopped in horror. All he could see of his brother was a shoe, upside down, a gray sock underneath it, and a shin and knee, badly scratched. The rest of Roger had crashed heavily into the bramble bush and had been eagerly clutched and held fast by the wicked, tearing thorns. Roger was gasping, almost crying with pain, and Stephen quickly began the difficult task of releasing him.

"All right, Rog. Now hold still—I'll get you out. Gosh, brother, you've really done a beautiful job on that gate, and your trousers . . ."

"Curse the gate!" came a muffled yell from Roger. "The rotten farmer ought to keep his gates better repaired, then I shouldn't—ow! Crikey!" He squealed. "I can't move without tearing myself to bits. Come on—get me up!"

"It's all right, Rog," Stephen said, as he began pulling the brambles aside. "I'll clear these away from your legs, then lift you up. . . ."

Luckily he had a penknife with him and was able to cut off most of the briars, so that soon Roger's bottom half was clear of thorns. Stephen cut, pulled, bent, and kicked the briars out of the way, with many a squeal from

Roger as bendy brambles whipped back, unwilling to release their victim. As more and more of the bush was cleared away, the more the damage to Roger and his clothes became apparent. The wool of both his socks had caught badly on the thorns and had pulled out in great lengths as he had wriggled and squirmed. Stephen, too, by this time was badly scratched all over his hands and arms, and his temper was fraying, even though he knew that he simply must keep on and get Roger out—and quickly.

"Blast the thorns! Oh, blast!" Stephen was almost crying with vexation now and beginning to feel furiously angry with his younger brother for getting them both into such a painful mess. He kept bending back, cutting, kicking savagely at the briars until at last he was able to pull the yelling Roger clear of the fatal bush and sprawl him across the grass of the meadow. "There, you silly fool. I hope that'll teach you not to climb rotten old gates. Look at my hands!"

"Look at my trousers!" sobbed Roger. "Look at my coat and my shirt, and my socks, and my arms, and my legs, and my face . . . I'm sore all over. Every square inch of me is sore. I'll probably die of blood poisoning. . . ." He lay still on his side, groaning and gasping, clutching his bottom.

Stephen's anger had faded now that the horrible job of tearing the brambles apart had been overcome. He began to feel sorry that he had been so foul to Roger. The poor boy looked dreadful. There were four or five vicious scratches right across his face. A particularly deep one across his right cheek and ear was bleeding steadily, and Roger's frequent rubbing of his hand tenderly across his sore face was quickly spreading out the blood and giving him a ghastly, blood-soaked look. His hands and arms, too, had taken a terrible, tearing punishment. And his clothes! Stephen whistled in dismay at the rip in Roger's jacket, three separate tears on the front of his shirt, and his tattered socks. He took out a handkerchief and began wiping the blood from Roger's face. They could not go any further on their ride looking like that. People—if they met anyone—would think someone had tried to murder Roger, and Stephen himself felt the dirtiest and untidiest he had ever felt in his life—and certainly the sorest.

When at last Roger felt recovered enough to get up, they both walked down the sloping field to where a tiny stream trickled along in a miniature valley. There, with Roger protesting, but Stephen insisting, scratches were washed and wiped and dabbed until all but the worst had stopped bleeding and the boys at last looked more like boys and not "raw meat," which Roger kept saying he felt like. Stephen's bloodstained handkerchief was given a final rinse in the stream, wrung out until it was nearly dry, and then given to Roger to hold against the bad scratch which still oozed blood down his cheek.

It was a painful walk up the sloping grass and over the wrecked gate. But it was when the boys picked up their bikes and began riding that the real soreness began. Stephen felt his hands sore on the handgrips, his wrists and arms tingling angrily as the wind and his sleeve rubbed against the scratches. But Roger! They had gone only a dozen yards when Roger called out, "It's no good, Steve. I can't ride like this. I shall come off. Hang on a minute." He dabbed his sore cheek again with the wet handkerchief, wriggled his arms painfully inside his sleeves and felt gingerly behind him. "Gosh, I've scratched my bottom in about five thousand places. No wonder I can't keep on the seat. And there's a rip a mile wide, look, Steve. I can't go about with my shirt hanging out like this!"

Stephen chuckled. "You certainly can't walk like that. Riding is the only way to cover up your wounded rear! Come on. Get on and try again. Think of the girls and those sizzling sausages!"

They came to the main road, and soon Roger was lagging behind. Stephen stopped at the top of the hill and waited for his brother. Across the road to his right the ground fell away again gradually, through a wide field full of sheep, until it came to a dark-green mass of trees whose tops were level with his view.

That must be a deep little valley down there, he was thinking, when Roger came level with him, gasping and puffing. Stephen had his foot on the pedal ready to push off and continue the ride when Roger snapped, "Hang on a minute, Steve. I can't go on like this. That bramble bath was awful. My legs are shocking sore, and pedaling makes it worse—my trousers rub on the scratches. It's jolly painful. Can't we stop a minute?"

"Stop? We'll be late, even if we hurry," Stephen said

angrily. "You'll have to put up with sore legs. We've got to get there before the girls, so come on!"

"No, I can't. It's awful. You'll have to go on by yourself. My legs really are rotten. Look, my trousers are making 'em bleed again," he said, groping in his pocket for a handkerchief. He pulled it out and dabbed it on the reddening scratches. "Honest, Steve. I just can't pedal any more with these rotten scratches. I'll have to freewheel downhill and then walk uphill, so you'd better go on by yourself. There's no need to wait for me. I'll meet you at the quarry."

"O.K." Stephen sighed. "If you really can't, you can't."

He got out the map and pointed the way again, to make sure his brother knew where to go. He was just about to pack the map away when Roger said, "Hey, hang on. Look—this line here—what does this mean?" He pointed to the map. Stephen looked and said, "That's a sort of minor road, probably just a farm road, down to those houses there. Then it peters out to a footpath through those woods. Why?"

"Well, look," said Roger excitedly. "That'd take us nearly direct to where we want to go. Down that road, on that footpath through those woods—that straight bit— then we're there. Why not go that way?"

"You can't, Rog," said his brother impatiently. "This first bit's all right, but the footpath's no good to cycle on. It'd be all bumpy, across the side of a plowed field maybe."

"There aren't any plowed fields here," objected Roger.

"Well, across a field, anyway. And it'd wind all through the trees and—"

"It shows it straight enough on the map," put in Roger.

"Yes, but it can't show all the little twists and bends on a small map like this. It's no good. The main road'll be much quicker," Stephen said.

"I'm going to try it, anyway," said Roger.

"You're what?" gasped Stephen.

"It's a lot shorter. I'm going that way," Roger repeated, and he added rather wildly, "and I'll beat you there. Give us a look at the map. . . ."

In spite of Stephen's pleading, Roger was obstinate. He felt rather pleased with himself for seeing on the map this new way across country. He was quite sure it would be an easier and much quicker route. He also felt faintly afraid, yet thrilled, at the thought of venturing into unknown territory by himself. In the end Stephen decided that he had better give Roger the map. He said grumpily, "Well, if you must be pigheaded. But don't go and get lost so that we all have our picnic and everything spoiled by having to look for you. Come on. The turning down that farm road can't be far ahead of us."

They freewheeled down the slope. Again the wind on his legs made the soreness worse, but now Roger had something to take his mind off his scratches. Near the top of the next slope Stephen, still well in the lead, stopped at the entrance to a farm roadway. It was a straight, narrow road, with low, well-trimmed hedges on each side. Down the left-hand side marched some telephone posts, at the far end of the track a gray group of buildings could be seen; beyond them lay a dark, low mass of woods stretching far to the right and left, filling the valley, which fell away just beyond the buildings. Very far away, beyond the woods, the sunlit fields could faintly be seen, rising up past the distant slopes of the valley.

Somewhere over those sunlit fields is where he will have to go, thought Stephen. Phew! He'll never find his way. But Roger, again appealed to as he at last came up to his brother, stoutly maintained that he would.

Roger now felt a new confidence in his map reading, and waved aside his brother's advice and offer of the map with an airy, "Pooh! I can see that all right. Snip. I'll be there before you. Look, meet you there—that little wood." He stabbed a finger down. "Hilltree Clump. See it? O.K? You'd better get a move on, Steve. Cheerio!"

Roger jumped on his bike and was well down the narrow road before Stephen could bring himself to set off on his separate way. Pedaling hard down the hilly road, he felt the wind in his face and the bicycle vibrating beneath him, heard the tires humming and his gears clicking smoothly, and forgot everything else in the thrill of riding fast. He felt free at last. Nothing more to stop him. Now he'd move! And as he thought of the day ahead, he suddenly felt ravenously hungry. As his legs pumped up and down, he breathed in time with them, "Sausages, sausages, sausages . . ."

3
Roger Alone

In the kitchen of the old farmhouse a boy was sitting, drinking cocoa. He was twelve years old but short and wiry so that he looked younger. His feet were swinging inches off the floor as he lifted the big half-pint willow-pattern mug and sipped.

"Now, Mark," said the woman at the sink. "Don't keep your mum waiting too long for these eggs. Maybe she'll want 'em for her cooking this morning. Sip your cocoa up, there's a good 'un."

"O.K., Auntie, but it's 'ot." Mark reached over to the table and took a second big, roughly round, homemade biscuit from the tin, and nibbled and sipped. His aunt was busy cutting up rutabagas for dinner, and his eyes lifted past her to the window she was facing. Big white fleecy clouds were floating across the sky. He had to squint, it was so bright out there after the dark old kitchen. He nibbled his biscuit, and then stopped in surprise. A boy flashed by on a bicycle, down the path just outside the kitchen window.

What was that across the boy's face? It looked like lines across his cheeks. War paint? Red Indians on bicycles? Mark chuckled to himself, hurriedly put down his cocoa, and flung himself out of the kitchen door. What was that boy on the bike up to? Was he lost? There was no road much, farther on.

Mark ran up the path from the door to the road and looked toward the woods. He could just see the boy wobbling rather badly as he disappeared out of sight toward the distant hedge and gate down the fields. Knowing that the bike could not get much farther, Mark set off down the path to follow.

Where's 'e 'eaded for, this way? he wondered.

Roger was quite unaware that he had aroused a pursuer. He had been too intent on keeping his balance. The lane surface was pitted with potholes and made it a rattly ride until he came to the gate. But he'd had two spills that day and did not intend to have a third.

He found the gate opened easily and pushed his bicycle through with one hand, and then fastened the gate with his other. The farmer, he thought, might let his lane get a bit worn, but his gates swung and shut cleanly enough.

Roger jumped onto his cycle and pedaled fast along the slightly downward path. He looked ahead and saw the next gate a hundred yards off. Past the gate was the mass of trees he had seen far off from the main road. They were much nearer now but still seemed low down. He could still look across their tops, a smooth, dark sea of slight movement, with some dark green cones of fir tops sticking out above. He wondered how steep the path would be when he got into the trees and down to the stream.

He came up to the second gate, went through it, and saw that the next field was sprinkled with sheep and lambs. As he began riding again down the more steeply downhill path, an old ewe rocketed away from nearby, stopped after four rapid steps and stood gazing at him, the lambs around her following and watching the boy on the bike. Roger saw that the lambs were numbered. These four had gotten 225, 104, 25, and . . . he missed the fourth as it jumped away, its black face pushed into the fleece of the ewe. All over the field there were hundreds of such groups—a ewe and a few lambs. Some were sprawled on the grass, some grazing, some standing and gazing. Far off, from the direction of the woods below, came the bark of a dog.

Quite suddenly the field began sloping downward very steeply. Roger soon decided that he had better get off and walk. Again he heard barking ahead of him. It seemed to come from just inside the woods. He was getting close to the gate where the path left the field and entered the trees. He was much lower down now, in a quite steep little valley. He could no longer look across the tops of the trees. He was near enough, when he could risk taking his eyes off the steep, stony path, to see the densely packed trunks of the bare trees towering high above him. He was near enough to catch the occasional tinkling of water in some nearby brook. There came the furious dog-barks again, just ahead.

Then immediately in front of Roger a tiny lamb dashed out of the woods, through a gap in the wire netting and up toward him. Close behind, yapping furiously, came a big black-and-white collie dog. It caught the lamb with mouth and paw. Roger, horrified, saw the tiny lamb squirming helplessly and bleeding from a bite on its side. He flung down his bike and launched himself toward the big dog, waving his arms and shouting wildly, "Gerrout of it, gerraway! Shoo!" and kicking angrily till the beast let go of the lamb and turned snarling toward him.

With teeth bared, the dog crouched and dodged Roger's wild kicks, intended to frighten it away rather than really to kick it. It seemed to sense this and turned again to the lamb, still only a yard away and now bleating piteously. Roger saw the dog's intention and kicked out again. This time he landed a good right-footer on the furious animal's shoulder. It swerved from the lamb, barking madly, and this gave Roger just enough time to snatch up the terrified lamb and tuck it under his jacket, wrapping the folds lightly around the quivering little body, which at first wriggled wildly and then went still. The dog jumped at Roger, who, needing both arms to hold his coat shut over the lamb, could only kick and shout. The collie seemed angrier with each leap; and when finally one

huge bound took it fiercely crashing against Roger's side, nearly knocking the lamb out of his grasp, Roger felt a wave of panic sweep over him. There was no one anywhere near . . . . The dog was going mad.

He saw his bike on the ground a few paces away and dashed over to it, wobbling oddly on the slope, with his frightened burden. The poor lamb now started struggling again, and it took all Roger's strength and balance to hold it still, kick out at the collie, and quickly bend over his bike and grab the pump.

He turned just as the dog jumped up at his chest. Its teeth, snapping at the lamb's terrified head, caught the coat instead and ripped the cloth from top to bottom. This infuriated Roger so much—he had not had the jacket long—that his panic was lost in a wave of anger, and he lashed out with his pump. He was holding it by the top and, as he swung, it slid out to its full extent, catching the collie a mighty blow across the head. The beast whimpered and kept its distance, watching the weapon which Roger now brandished in front of it.

This was better. Roger felt his panic subsiding. If only the lamb would stop wriggling! What had he better do? Stay there and yell for help while keeping the dog at bay with his pump—or try to make his way back up the sloping field and then see if anyone was around to help him? He decided that it was no good at all staying there and yelling. There was no one for miles, he was sure. So he began backing carefully up the slope. It was difficult, for he had to hold the wriggling lamb inside his jacket with his left hand, wave the pump at the dog with his right, and watch both lamb and dog, which left him nothing but two weary and badly scratched legs to get up the slope with.

He stepped back—one foot, then the other. The dog immediately snarled and moved forward. Roger stepped back too hurriedly and sat down hard. The lamb squirmed convulsively and Roger almost let go.

"Hold still, you silly beggar! I'm trying to save you! Hold still!" Roger growled. He clenched his aching left arm more firmly across his coat, squeezing the palpitating little body tight against his shirt, and slowly stood up. The collie barked furiously. Roger waved the pump and was delighted and surprised to see the dog turn and scurry away down the slope to the fence, through the gap and out of sight into the woods.

Feeling almost gay with relief, Roger turned and was about to start his walk back up the hill when he saw why the dog had fled. A boy was racing down the field, and behind him was a big, burly farmworker, loping along. They both had sticks in their hands and were clearly just the sort to deal with lamb-biting dogs.

Again Roger sat down. His knees suddenly felt weak and wobbly. He stroked the lamb's head as it nuzzled out of his jacket, and said, "It's O.K., lamb. You're safe enough now. Nasty bowwow's gone." Then he grinned to himself and thought how daft he was, talking to the animal just as he used to talk to Tim when he was a baby.

The boy panted up to him. "You all right?"

"Yes, I'm O.K. But the dog bit this lamb," said Roger.

The beefy man arrived. "Hello, sonny. That damn dog having a go at you?"

36

The other boy said, "No, Jim. It's been arter the lambs again. He's got 'un under his jacket."

"I'm afraid it's bitten the lamb too. I couldn't get to it in time. Is it going to be all right?" Roger lifted the tiny thing out of his coat and put it into the great red hands of the man.

The man looked it over, whistled when he saw the gash in the lamb's side, and swore. "We atter shoot that dog. Alb 'Erratt's again, I'll bet. That's the third lamb this week's been bit. Other two died, but this'll be O.K." He looked at Roger and smiled. "Good lad. But you look as though it bit you too. Come on, back to the house, and let's get you cleaned up. You gotta have something on them scratches."

They walked the two field lengths back, and on the way the other boy explained.

"I see you whiz past on your bike and followed. Me shoelace come loose, else I'd 'ave caught up with you sooner, but when I heard that dog a-yelping I forgot you. I thought it were the sheep again, so I called Jim."

"Yes, lucky I were working on that bit o' wall," Jim put in. "I reckon Alb 'Erratt probably broke that gap in it too," he grumbled. "Night afore last he were out in the woods around here, I reckon."

"I'm jolly glad you came when you did," Roger admitted. "I gave that dog a whack with my pump, but I didn't know what to do really."

They arrived at the farmhouse. Jim handed the lamb over to another man and then knocked on the door and went in. He hurriedly brushed aside the horrified exclamations of the woman in the kitchen, Mark's aunt, and said, "Now, Mrs. Gray, it's nothing much, but can you clean this lad up a bit? He's had a go with an ol' dog—probably Alb Herratt's collie, I reckon—and he's got a bit of blood off the lamb on his shirt. Blasted dog nipped the lamb's side." He added rather puzzledly, "He's got a lot of scratches on him, though."

Mrs. Gray hurriedly led Roger over to the sink. "You poor boy!" she exclaimed. "Whatever have you been up to? Did the dog do all these?" She wiped as she spoke, with a washcloth quickly dipped into antiseptic and water. "Oh, they do look sore." She did both his arms, his knees, and exclaimed again at the sight of Roger's chest when she had pulled open his tattered and bloodstained shirt. "Here, sit down now." She pulled a chair up close to the sink. "Your coat! And shirt! Whatever will your mother say? Did that dog do all these?"

Roger squirmed as she wiped the blood off his chest and side. A lot of sticky blood from the lamb had soaked through his shirt, and now the water from the washcloth trickled down and ran inside the top of his trousers.

The man had picked up the tattered jacket Roger had taken off. "Did ol' dog do this too?" he asked, holding up the loose flap of the torn top pocket.

"Yes, it jumped up at the lamb and . . ."

"Cor!" said Mark. "Ol' dog didn't like you, did 'un?"

Roger smiled ruefully and said, "No, I don't think it did."

Five minutes later he was sitting by the table, sipping

hot tea and crunching homemade biscuits. His scratches had all been bathed. At first they had been sore, but now they felt better, all except the bad ones across his cheek. He had explained how he had become so scratched, had told about the dog and the lamb and his swipe with the pump, and now sat watching Mrs. Gray hurriedly stitching up the tear in his jacket.

When she had finished, she said, "There. It's not a real neat job, but it's really too bad for my mending. Still, it looks like a coat again and not an old scarecrow's rag!" She smiled and said, "I'm sorry I can't do anything about the shirt in time for you, but I'll wash it and send it on. You write your name and address down here." She passed him an old envelope and watched him write. "Ah," she said, picking it up. "Roger Fern. I'm sure my hubby will be very grateful to you. You're a good lad, saving that liddle lamb from Alb 'Erratt's dog. You sure you can't wait and have dinner with us and see Mr. Gray when he comes in?" But Roger had already explained that he must really go, so reluctantly she did not press him.

He stood up. He was wearing the other boy's jersey instead of a shirt, and it felt tickly. Still, it was decent of the boy to lend it. He had suggested it, in fact, when he had seen how hopelessly bloody Roger's shirt was. Roger took the mended jacket and put it on. He thanked the woman politely and picked up his pump. "Must've given it a good headache—that collie." He smiled ruefully. He had now noticed that the pump's plunger part had a distinct bend. It was pretty hard to pull it out, or push it in. He tried again. No, it would not be much good as a pump again. But it had done fine as a weapon in his hour of need.

Mrs. Gray, however, was concerned. "You bent it, giving that ol' dog a whack? Then you shall have a new pump. Here." She took a jar from the shelf over the fireplace and picked out two half-crowns. "You buy yourself a new one. She pressed the money into Roger's hand, and bustled him and Mark out of the kitchen. "You'll be late for those sausages if you don't get a move on. You go with Roger, Mark, as far as the Stones and show him the way. Tell your mum and dad I'll send your shirt on when I've washed it. And come and see us again next time you come this way. Good-bye now. Mark— don't be too long. Your mum'll be wondering where you and them eggs are. It's nearly twelve." She waved as they left the farmyard.

Roger said to Mark, "Gosh! Nearly twelve already! Come on, I'm late. I'd nearly forgotten those girls and Stephen." He hurried on, and explained to Mark again about his cousins, the meeting with Stephen at Hilltree Clump, the car ride from Cambridge, the sausages . . .

The two boys began to run, Roger worrying about the time, Mark thinking enviously that he wished he had brothers and cousins. He wondered if he could join in this game and go on with Roger. No, his mum was waiting for the eggs. He ran on down the field, shouting, "Mind them potholes. You'm bashed about enough already!"

4

The Bristolites

By nine o'clock that morning the boys' cousins in Bristol, Sarah and Jane Barr, were up, had made their beds, had helped their mother with packing up the picnic food, had loaded the folding chairs into the car, had perused the map of the district around the picnic quarry many times, and had said at least four times each, "Mum, do you think it's going to rain?" They had been patiently reassured at least four times each, had run to the shop down the hill for an extra bottle of pop, and finally had had to sit fuming, waiting for their father to return from an emergency call to the hospital.

So it was nearer twelve than eleven when they came to

the bridge at Windford, two miles from the picnic rendezvous.

There Jane and Sarah, who had been whispering over
the map in the back of the car, persuaded their father not
to drive direct to Pine Tree Quarry but to divert a little
so that they could get out and cut across the fields.

"We know the way, and it'll be a change," said Sarah.

Neither girl would explain further, but clearly something was being plotted. Mary was nearly in tears at being
left behind when the car stopped in a side road and her
sisters got out. They skipped across the edge of the road
and were over the gate and away into the field, scattering
sheep and their lambs in their hurry.

"Our daughters aren't usually so keen on running, are
they?" commented a rather puzzled Dr. Barr as he swung
the car around, back toward the picnic rendezvous.

"No—something they've planned with the boys, I
guess," said his wife. "At least now they've gone we can
spread out in the car for a few minutes." She allowed
Peter to scramble over into the back seat. "Watch him,
Mary. Don't let him start opening the food tins."

Stephen was grunting with the effort of pedaling up
the steep bridle path. He had made good time since
leaving Roger. The main road had been quiet, the side
road empty, and the village he had to go through had been
no problem. He had remembered the map, had crossed
the brook at the far side of the village—and had turned
up the second opening on the right. But he had not read

the map as far as imagining the slope of this bridle way! It was steep! His legs ached awfully, but he felt sure he was riding faster than he could walk, so he forced himself to keep on. About half a mile more, he judged, and then, as he passed a group of barns on his right, the slope lessened. He was at the edge of the little plateau and his object, Hilltree Clump, was straight ahead. He could see no one there waiting. His heart thumped even faster. He panted, gasped, pedaled furiously the last few score of yards, threw down his cycle and stood, happily puffing, at the bend in the path. He was first there. He could see no one coming from the sloping fields by which he guessed Roger would approach, from the woods down there to his right. Stephen sighed happily. Not long now before the sausages would be on his hungry fork.

He had been sitting with his back against a tree, looking up the path, willing Roger to appear for nearly twenty minutes when he suddenly sat up in surprise and saw not one, but two figures hurrying toward him in the distance. He squirmed out of sight, made sure his bicycle was hidden, and then kept watch cautiously through the trees. He was startled to see Jane and Sarah, only fifty yards away. What on earth were they doing here? How did they know. . . ? He thought of letting them go past and remaining hidden but decided against it. They might have news of Roger. He stood up and stepped out into the pathway. The two trotting girls came to a startled halt.

"Wow! Steve! You scared me!" gasped Jane. She turned to Sarah and grinned. "We were right. Up to some devilish plot, those Ferns are!"

"Yes, but where's Roger? Still in hiding?" Sarah plunked herself down on the grass and sat, puffing slightly, against a welcome tree trunk. "Have you sent him off to keep lookout or. . . ?"

"No, he hasn't got here yet. But what are you doing here? How'd you know we'd be here? And haven't you seen Rog?" Stephen was a little bewildered.

But the two Bristolites could not help; Jane explained that they had expected the boys to remember their threat to get even with them after the April Fools' Day trick, and they had guessed that they would do something about avoiding falling into a trap at the quarry. "We looked at the map and wondered where you'd start from to reach the picnic place another way," explained Sarah. "And we reckoned you'd go from somewhere near Upton village and cut across the fields."

"So we told Dad to come around this way, got out of the car at the main road back there, and were going to aim across the fields to get there before you," put in Jane.

"Only Daddy was so blessed late again that he's messed it all up, and we're too late by miles," sighed Sarah. "So our revenge will have to wait."

"Then you haven't seen Roger?" Stephen was still anxious but warmly appreciative of his cousins' brains. He and Rog had expected a counterattack. Jane and Sarah had expected them to expect it and so had planned something else. He wondered what they had up their sleeves. But first there was Roger. Where was the young idiot?

He explained to the girls how he had separated from Roger. They did not seem to think there was anything to be alarmed about.

"He can't be long now. It isn't all that far. Let's wait for him," said Sarah, quite content to sit against her tree and bask in the brightening sunshine.

Wait they did, until their stomachs insisted that waiting any longer was pointless, that Roger had surely found another way to the picnic, and that they had better hurry to get there too.

"Before he and those greedy beasts Mary and the twins eat everything," said Jane.

Stephen did not like abandoning the wait, but he could not better the girls' argument. He was feeling ravenous too and persuaded himself he did not believe his brother could have come to any real harm.

"Right! Let's be going," he agreed, standing up at last. "And if he's not there soon, that's hard luck. I'm hungry enough to eat his share as well!"

5

Roger Again

"What did your aunt mean by 'as far as the Stones'?" Roger puffed, hurrying for the second time down the steep, sheep-clad slopes of Mr. Gray's fields toward the brook. Mark, trotting wordlessly along in front, stopped, clambered up the gate they had just reached and said, "The Stones across the river—down there—in the woods. That's the best way to Hilltree if you'm in 'urry. You'll 'ave to walk though. Can't bike that way. It's steep, other side the brook."

"Oh," said Roger doubtfully. "My bike's down here where I dropped it. I suppose I shall have to leave it."

"No, I'll take it back for you to me auntie's," said

Mark. "She won't mind. I'll put it in the barn. Your dad can bring you right down to the house, and you can get the bike then, on your way back 'ome."

"Thanks!" said Roger. "That's fine." They came to the bike, and as Roger bent to fit his ruined pump into its brackets—it fitted much more tightly now that the handle was bent—he glanced anxiously toward the woods. But all was quiet. Sheep were everywhere and their bleating filled the air with a continual fugue of baas, but there were no barks this time. Roger straightened up. Where had the collie gone? Who was Alberrutt? Where did he live? At the thought of the man's name Roger felt a queer uneasiness start inside him. Peculiar name, he thought. "Alberrutt"—that's how everyone says it. Queer name. Must be a queer man—with a fierce dog and a habit of breaking gaps in stone walls at night, apparently.

"Ready, then?" Mark's voice brought Roger back to the present, and he grinned quickly. "Yes, let's go. Thanks about the bike," he said.

They reached the gate at the edge of the woods. Over its green, creaking bars both boys climbed, and Mark led the way along the narrow overhung path, which turned sharp right at once.

The wood was very still. All sound seemed deadened there, and both boys became quiet, moving almost surreptitiously. Roger remembered a book about a policeman getting lost in a woods. The man had felt that lots of little eyes were watching him. Some big ones had been too, Roger thought and grinned, for his clothes had all been pinched when he went for a swim in the Blind Pool. But that's what it felt like here, still and secret.

The trees were bare in their early springtime habit—only a few holly leaves among all the gray and green and silver trunks, only a few green shoots among the rotting brown leaves which carpeted the ground. Everywhere looked unused to humans, except the path. That was clear enough, not at all overgrown. That would be Alberrutt—and his dog—Roger guessed apprehensively. They would be up and down this path every night and some of the day.

They had gone about a quarter of a mile along the narrow track when the path turned sharp left and the sound of rippling water became louder. Then the trees thinned, the ground fell steeply for twenty grassy feet, and Roger saw the river gleaming in front of him.

The sun was directly in front of him, shining brilliantly through the slender silver birches that climbed up the other bank. Roger was dazzled. The sunlight on the water was blinding. It was well after twelve and a long time after he ought to have met Stephen, but he had forgotten that for the moment. He was thrilled by the beautiful spot Mark had brought him to. Mark was at the bottom of the slope, standing on the first of the stepping-stones, calling something. Roger did not hear. He looked around him, shading his eyes. It was marvelous, just like a glade in Narnia, he thought, remembering the books read to him in his Junior School. The grass carpeting the ground so finely, with such a wonderful green, the slender, graceful, silvery boles of the birch trees, the dappled blue of the water, the white stones, the blue sky and clouds fleecy white, except for one big black one. Surely this was the finest place in the world? Roger was not usually liable to notice a pretty view. He could not understand his parents' enthusiasm for their garden, their thrill at a colorful flower border or rosebed. But this was really pure Narnia. He wondered how many people knew this spot. Then he heard Mark calling. "What? Oh yes, I'm coming," he said, and trotted down the grassy slope to the stepping-stones.

Mark was pointing at the mud near the first stone. Roger felt a thrill of alarm as he saw a dog's print, clear and recent.

"Looks like that ol' dog come back this way and went across here. Hope you don't meet 'im again, eh?" Mark grinned.

"Oh, I don't care." Roger sounded braver than he felt. "It won't bother me on my own. It was the lamb it was after."

"Maybe," Mark said. "You see where the path goes left, the other side there?" He pointed across the stream. "Up there through them rocks, till you get out o' the wood, across the meadows and you'll see Hilltree. You'll never make it by twelve though."

"No," said Roger. He stepped onto the first stone. "One thing, my scratches don't hurt so much now, except this one on my face. And thanks for the jersey—Mum'll send it back. And thanks for seeing to my bike. Good-bye, Mark."

"Good-bye—and good luck."

There were five stones in the river and a big long one at the far edge of the water. Roger ran across easily, stopped just long enough on the last one to look for and find a dog's pawmark in the mud, and turned to look again at the patch of New Narnia he had found. Yes, it was real. He waved back at Mark. "Bye!" he shouted again, and turned and began climbing the path. It wound this way and that, twisting wherever a tree or a rock—and there were plenty of both—got in the way. Roger clambered up, thinking how daft he had been to dream of bringing a bike up this sort of slope, over this sort of rock.

He was nearly at the top, just getting ready to see what the wood ahead was like, when a sudden flurry of dog-barks not very far off made him slip in alarm. He stopped. His heart was beating wildly. The barks came again. They were nearer, he was sure, and there—a man's voice. The rough shouts came clearly, mingled with the dog's yelps. Roger felt panic rising in him. It was the same dog—and Alberrutt too. They were just ahead. If he went on, he would run straight into them. He ought to go on. He had done nothing wrong. He had every right to go on. He turned and ran in terror back down to the river.

It was silly to run down such a slope. After only a few huge slithering steps Roger fell and rolled into a clump of bushes near the long flat stone by the river's edge. Luckily the bushes were hazel, not holly. He had fallen nastily, and his left ankle hurt. His heart beating wildly, he stood up and looked back through the trees. He felt a new wave of fear sweep over him. A man and a dog were coming down the path!

Roger was across the stepping-stones in a flash. One, two, three, four, squelch! He had missed the last stone. His left foot again! He tugged it clear of the clinging mud, which eddied into the sparkling water. His foot came painfully out, and so did his sock, torn by brambles, snagged on the rocky path and now nearly off his foot—but no shoe. He was in such a panic that he hardly noticed it was missing. More barks snarled behind him. He tumbled, sobbing, straight up the bank. He had no thoughts of New Narnia now.

At the top of the slope Roger found that his ankle was hurting him. He knew he could never get back to the gate and up the fields again to Mr. Gray's farmhouse before that awful dog and the even awfuller Alberrutt caught him and . . . He shuddered. No, he would have to get off the path and hide. He came to where the path turned sharp right and struck off to the left through the trees and holly bushes, which were thickly grouped there. How far could a dog scent you? He did not know.

He went farther and farther into the woods, away from the path, to make sure he was out of sight and out of scent. He crossed a tiny clearing, limping now, for his ankle was becoming painful, worse by far now that he had no shoe on it, and there he found a half-fallen tree.

It was a big birch, taller than the rest of its neighbors, and therefore had been caught by the wind one stormy day. It had half uprooted itself, but no more, for it had

fallen straight into the fork of another tree. There it
rested, still growing, sloping like an aimed missile, with
a huge hole beneath it, where part of its roots had torn
away. It made a natural hiding place. Roger scrambled
into the hole, brushing aside a small holly bush carelessly
with his arm. More scratches, and a snag in the cuff of the
jersey of Mark's he was wearing, but he was past caring.
The wet sock on his left foot slipped off his heel. He
pulled it right off.

The hole was fine, just the sort of place to disappear
into, but it surprised Roger by being much deeper than
he had expected. If he wanted to, he could stand on a

tiny ledge so that he was hidden from the waist down, but this was not good enough. The holly bush did not cover the hole entrance fully. Roger carefully stretched out his left leg, the barefooted one, and lowered it backward, trying to find another step. He was about to give up and draw his aching ankle upward and make do with crouching lower on the step where he was, when his toe touched something smooth and firm and broad and cold. Then he quickly cowered down, holding his breath, all his terrors renewed.

A rough, loud voice boomed across the floor of the woods, level with Roger's head, and the excited barks of the dog hurried nearer. Just as Roger was expecting the dog to be almost upon him and to ferret him out of his hiding place, the man's voice broke into a flood of cursing that brought Roger's hair up on end. "Come 'ere, you blurry'ound! You . . . ! Bab! 'Ere! Get out o' that!" And with the last shout there came the whizzing of a stone, a crack as it hit a tree trunk, and a startled yelp from the dog.

Roger felt weak with relief as the sounds of dog and angry man grew fainter and faded along the path away from him. He found he was trembling slightly. He could not remember when he had been afraid like that before. And he was cold. It was more than cool in this cave under the tree roots: it was freezing. His foot was aching and felt icy. He touched the bare foot and ankle. It hurt by the bone—and his foot was wet. He rubbed his hand under his heel and sole again and then looked at his hand. There was no mud, just clean wetness on his fingers. Oh well, so there was a flat wet stone down there. It didn't matter. He had to get back to the path and start out once more to meet Stephen and the girls. Gosh, how many times was it that he'd started out already? It must be awfully late, and getting a fright really had made him terrifically hungry.

Roger shifted his feet so as to get a good firm kick off for his jump out of the hidey-hole. He was about to leap upward when under his bare toes he felt something loose. He bent down and felt one round, smooth thing. Roger picked it up. He was stooping right down into the cave now. His coat must be getting a bit of a mess from the roots and the soil but—then he gasped. From the smooth, round thing in his hand there came a gleam as he straightened up and held it in the light. It was a large, heavy coin. It was clean and shining, and it looked like gold.

"Gosh!" he gasped.

He turned the coin over. On one side was a clean raised profile of a bearded man with a faint, worn, laurel wreath on the back of his head. On the reverse side was a woman's figure, sitting on a sort of stool with a shield by her left hand and a spear in her right. Britannia? wondered Roger. No, couldn't be, for clear, below the woman's figure, where the date usually is on a penny, was the word *ROMA*.

It had always been one of Roger's ambitions to own a Roman coin. Now it looked as if he had found one at last. Could it be a Julius Caesar coin? Julius was Roger's hero in Roman history. But, no. When he looked at the side of the coin where the head was, there was no Julius printed around the edge, but something that looked like *NEROCLAUDIAES . . . GERM . . . T*. The letters were not very clear in places and Roger could not make much of it. He vaguely thought that perhaps there had been an emperor called Nero, but . . .

He put the coin into his pocket, the back trouser pocket, because he knew his others had holes in them. The coin clinked against the two half-crowns Mrs. Gray had made him have for a new pump, then he knelt down carefully. He had better see, or rather feel, if there were any more coins lying there. His hand brushed across the smooth surface he was standing on. There was no other coin, but there did seem to be lines all over the stone, or whatever he was standing on. He reached as far as he could behind him, under the tree roots. He could just touch the edge of the stone and feel where the earth started again. He wriggled his fingers against the edge and felt a tiny piece come loose.

Roger stood up and looked at the tiny cube of stone he was holding. One side was a pale blue—and the others a sort of concrete color. It was not quite straight along all sides. Roger thrust this souvenir, too, into his back pocket. His foot was hurting again and felt very cold. He had messed about enough. He had better see if all was clear and then get on toward the quarry.

The wood was very still when he emerged from his hiding place. He pulled his sock onto his swollen foot. It was soaking and felt colder than ever, but even a sock would protect his foot a little. As he bent his foot up, he saw a pattern of little squares imprinted on his heel. He could not wait to puzzle that out, so he pulled the sock as far up as he could and started out again.

"Gosh," he almost wept to himself, "I hope I make it this time. Surely nothing can go wrong again!" He limped down to the stepping-stones to look for his shoe.

6
Pine Tree Quarry Picnic

When's Roger coming?" asked Tim for the fiftieth time. It was nearly two o'clock. When Stephen, Jane, and Sarah had joined the others at Pine Tree Quarry without Roger, there had been some little amusement that the surefire "shortcut" had not proved so short after all. As the girls had said before, there had been no need to worry about him. But now he really was overdue. About time we called out the lifeboat, thought Stephen miserably. The silly, silly beggar. What the pip was he doing?

The sun was blazing down from a sky that made everyone think summer was near. The grown-ups, Mr. and Mrs. Fern, Dr. and Mrs. Barr, were lying, half dozing in deck chairs, facing the April sun and soaking up its warmth. Dr. Barr, always ready to sunbathe at the slightest excuse, had taken his shirt off. The seven children were at the last stages of the picnic dinner. It was the time when someone would look around at the smeared plates, the scattered cups and beakers, the kettle singing on the campfire and sigh, "Well, we'd better do the washing up. Come on. Sooner we start, the quicker we begin."

Jane, being the oldest girl and therefore feeling responsible for the tidying-up operations, was just about to say these very words when Mrs. Fern said in a determined voice, "There, it's two o'clock. He's an hour late. Something must have happened to him. Come on, George and Stephen. We'd better backtrack and find him."

"All right. Point taken," groaned Mr. Fern, struggling up from his deck chair. "We'd better begin where you left him, Stephen. Show me on the map."

Stephen walked over to his bicycle. He was in a bitter mind. He was angry suddenly at Roger. They ought to be starting a game of cricket now, in the field at the top of the little quarry, not having to go charging off all over the countryside looking for silly idiots who got themselves lost. Blast Roger! he thought to himself. He's not safe out of his baby carriage. At the back of his mind he felt largely to blame, and that made him angrier. He ought never to have let Roger go off on his own. He should have gone with him, and then none of this would have happened.

"Silly blooming idiot," he grumbled as he spread out

the map. He pointed to where he had left his brother. "Look, it's only about two miles to where I met the girls. He must be daft to get lost as easily as that."

"Or hurt," his father quietly reminded him. "Some of these fields can be rough, and if he was in a hurry he may well have run into trouble."

That put the possibility squarely before the older children and the grown-ups. (The younger ones were either running, shrieking, around the trees and bushes, or gathering up wood for the endlessly hungry fire.) As anxiety spread, so did irritation. Soon the two older girls were in a furious squabble over the washing up, which ended up with cutlery slammed down onto the grass by a nearly frantic Sarah, who insisted that Jane was deliberately not putting the spoons straight enough in the rinsing water to be picked up all together. Clearly it was no good just waiting. Something active to break the tension had to be done. So Mrs. Barr, picking up the scattered spoons and forks, said, "Leave the rest for me to finish. Jane and Sarah can come with you, Stephen, and your dad, and look for Rog."

"Good idea," said Mrs. Fern. She collected the younger Barrs, Mary, Peter, and Anne, and Tim, and said, "Come on, let's go to the top of the quarry and see if we can see old Roger coming across the fields."

On top, past the bushes, the level grass was close-nibbled by the sheep and the wind blew freshly. It was not nearly so warm there as it had been in the sheltered scoop of the tiny hollow.

Mrs. Fern shaded her eyes with a hand and gazed hopefully across the sloping field. For about a quarter of a mile the slope was gentle. Then the grass fell steeply down to a line of trees whose tops just showed from the course of the river. Sheep were there by the score but no signs of her lost son.

"Shall we call him, Mummy?" suggested Tim. "If we all shout as loud as we can, he might hear us and know we're over here."

"Good idea, Tim," said his mother. "Ready, Mary and the twins?" They all five turned and faced the open field. "When I get to three, yell as hard as you can. One—two—three—Roger! And again. One—two—three—*Roger*! Last time. One—two—three—*ROGER*!"

"He must've heard that, Mummy," panted Tim. "He must've. When's he coming, Mummy?"

"I don't know, darling," said Mrs. Fern, with a catch in her voice. "But I expect it'll be soon now. Daddy's going to find him and—Oh!" She gasped as a boy stepped out from behind a hawthorn bush nearby and came toward them. "Who are you?"

He was nothing like Roger, who, in the first split second of seeing him, she had hoped he would be. He was smaller than Roger, but was perhaps older than he looked. His brown eyes were sparkling, and he looked quite excited about something.

" 'Scuse me, missis. You calling out like that—Roger, I mean—en't 'e got here yet?" the boy said.

"No, no, he hasn't," said Mrs. Fern shakily. "Do you know anything about him? Have you seen him? And where did you come from? And how did you know he was coming here?"

"I saw 'im afore I went back for me dinner. I don't know what time it was. Then there was that do with Alb 'Erratt's dog. Least, Jim thunk it were 'is, 'cause it's just the sort of trick you'd expect, but it en't certain. Then I took his bike to Auntie's, 'cause we all told him he'd never get a bike over them fields, not with all the stones, and stiles and all. But 'e ought to be 'ere by now. He said he were looking forward to the cricket game. You en't finished the cricket yet, 'ave you, missis? 'S a bit early for cricket, en't it? We're still playin' footer 'ere. Still that's no reason why you should. I been watchin', but all I see was eatin'." The boy looked down at the remains of the picnic below.

Mrs. Fern, utterly bewildered by this flood of words, at last took Mark down into the quarry, and there the four grown-ups, with occasional help from the fascinated children, pieced together the story Mark had to tell.

Mr. Fern summed it up. "So," he finally said, "you saw Roger ride by your aunt's house. You followed him and found him saving a lamb from a dog. You and your friend Jim the farmworker took Roger and the lamb back to your aunt's. Then you took him down to the river and showed him the way across by the stepping-stones, and that's the last you saw of him, at somewhere between half past twelve and one o'clock. You took his bike back to your aunt's for us to collect on the way home, and that's all you know?"

"Except he's got my jersey on," said Mark.

"Your jersey! Why?" exclaimed Mrs. Fern.

" 'Cause 'is was a bit torn, when the dog jumped up him, I reckon, so Auntie said she'd wash it and send it to 'im later. He didn't wanna keep my jersey on. He said it tickled. But the shirt was too messy—blood all over it—so he 'ad to. An' Auntie stitched up his jacket—and put some cream on the scratches on his leg, and—"

"Yes, yes," said Mr. Fern. "I see. So he's got your jersey on underneath his jacket, instead of a shirt. But where is he?"

"We'd better go to where I left him, Dad," said Stephen. "And perhaps Mark can show us where he saw him last. Then we'll go on from there. . . ."

"Right. That's what we'll do. That O.K. with you, Mark? Do you think your uncle will mind us searching over his fields?"

"No, 'e won't mind. 'E were proper pleased that Roger had saved that liddle lamb. I called in just as 'e was 'aving his dinner, on my way 'ere. Auntie had told him all about it, you see—and I expect he asked about the shirt she got, with blood all over it—'cause he wasn't there when Jim and me and Roger got back with the lamb. He said he were a good lad. 'E won't mind. Probably 'elp us look, unless he's gone to town about that wire 'e—"

"Right," Mr. Fern stopped the flood of words. The other children were gazing in wide-eyed astonishment at this new acquaintance of Roger's. How he talked—and talked—and talked! And wasn't it hard to know who the "he" was all the time? Jane thought.

Dr. Barr said, "Seems we'll all be useful if it's a search we've got to organize. Come on, you lot. Pack up the food. The two mums stay here to guard the camp—and in case Rog does turn up. All the rest, in our car, and let's get searching."

The two mothers needed some persuading but at last agreed to stay. Then the searchers all began to pile into Dr. Barr's big old Humber, that stood by the quarry gateway at the roadside. Dr. Barr, Mr. Fern, Tim, and Mark sat in the front so that Mark could be guide.

As her father was about to start the car, Sarah suddenly turned and rushed back to the picnic. She caught up with the others as they were cramming into the back seat. No one noticed that she now had a paper bag full of something in her hand. She, Jane, and Stephen had Mary, Anne, and Peter on their legs. "Cor," said Mark admiringly, as the car pulled out of the gateway and rolled down the hill. "With this lot we ought to find him, 'adn't we?"

But at first it certainly did not seem as if they would. Guided by Mark, they went quickly to his aunt's farmhouse, where Mrs. Gray was amused and delighted to see so many people unload from one car. Mr. Fern introduced himself and Dr. Barr and the children. He thanked Mrs. Gray for seeing to Roger's scratches and wanted to take his messy shirt, but she would not hear of it. "No. He saved that little lamb, and the least I can do is to wash his shirt for him," she insisted. "But whatever can have happened to him? You did show him the proper way, Mark, didn't you?"

"Course I did. He were going straight up the other side o' the brook last time I saw 'im," said Mark.

Mr. Fern suggested that they should walk down to the brook to see if they could trace the missing Roger—and perhaps Mark wouldn't mind going with them. They all set off across the home field and down the sloping pastures toward the brook.

Stephen, Jane, and Sarah thought how lovely it was to be strolling across such marvelous wide-open fields, springy turf under their feet, clear blue sky above their heads, a breeze just strong enough to be exciting but not enough to make the air cold, a good picnic dinner inside, and, Sarah thought to herself, the fun of looking for old Roger. She wondered if he had done it on purpose, to make the day more exciting, but she quickly let that thought go. Not so as to miss a picnic meal—not Roger.

The slope was so inviting that everyone began to run.

"Down that bottom, toward the next gate." Mark pointed as they all sat on the top of the second-to-last gate or on the fence by the side of it, getting their breath back.

"That's where Roger had the go with that ol' dog." Mark's words reminded them of their search, and the older children became quieter, thinking of Roger again and the puzzle of his disappearance. The younger ones, with little Tim in the lead, slipped off the gate and rushed eagerly down the field.

Stephen, Jane, and Sarah were in the rear now. "Looks pretty thick, this wood ahead," said Stephen. "If Roger strayed off the path, he'd find it hard going. Listen to that brook."

Clearly, as the wind blew gently toward them, came

64

the rushing, tumbling sounds of water, not far ahead and slightly to their left.

"Sounds like a big river," said Sarah.

"No, I guess it's just a small one fairly full up. We've had a lot of rain this last few weeks," Stephen said.

"Don't we know it!" exclaimed Jane. "We got soaked, waiting for the bus back from the swimming-baths yesterday."

They were at the end of the fields now. A sudden roar swept over their heads. Two planes with brilliant red noses swung low over the woods, climbing into the cloud-less sky. From the airfield up the road, Stephen guessed as he reached the gate.

"Right, Mark. Will you lead on and show us where you showed Roger over the river?" said Mr. Fern.

One by one they all followed Mark, climbing carefully over the rickety old gate. Mr. Fern felt Tim holding his hand tightly as they followed the path into the darkness of the thickly bunched trees. They suddenly noticed that the roaring of the river became less distinct as they went deeper into the woods. The path turned and led away from the sound and soon the splashing came only fitfully to them as the wind stirred capriciously among the bare birch trees. A second sharp turn, and the pitch brought them into the open glade by the river, the glade which the sun had lit up so magically for Roger, making him think of Narnia. Now, to the search party, most of them intent on their task, it looked just like any other part of the woods; a little more open, perhaps, with here and there a finer, bigger birch tree, but otherwise nothing special. But now the sun had lowered, and the glade was not bathed in midday yellow warmth. It was darkening green and gray, and the afternoon was hurrying on.

By the edge of the stream they all looked while Mark showed them where Roger had gone across. "Stepping-stones, Daddy. Can I go on them?" asked Tim, and soon everyone was crossing, following Tim, whose father held him firmly by the hand and had to lift him over the extra wide gap to the last stone, the big, wide landing slab.

There were six stepping-stones, so, with ten people to cross, it meant that the last one had to wait quite a while until the others had all started, since no stone was big enough for two people, and the two middle stones were hardly big enough for more than one foot.

Mary Barr was the last to cross, and while she waited for the others to go she noticed the movement of a stick in the stream near the bank where she was standing. She saw it float past the heel of Sarah's shoe, which for a second was on the first stone. Then it caught on the bank, came loose, and swirled on until it caught again and stuck. But what had it stuck on? Mary wondered. She bent closer and brought the line of stone-steppers to an immediate halt with her yell. "Hey, stop! I've found a shoe. Roger's shoe! It's got his name in it!"

She knelt down. She could just reach the shoe. She had to tug it quite hard to pull it out of the clinging mud. By the time she had tipped the icy cold water out of it, everyone else was gathered around her.

"Look, Uncle," she said, "It's got Roger's name in it."

She held it out, and Mr. Fern took the dripping shoe.

For a moment he looked serious, and then smiled and said cheerfully. "Fine. Clever girl, Mary. Hawkeye. That makes it a lot easier. He can't have got far without one shoe. We'll find him easily now. Careless young beggar. There's a pound's worth of shoe here. It's not all that old and he leaves it behind. I'll skin him!"

It was fortunate that neither Mr. Fern nor any of the others had a chance to begin wondering and worrying about how Roger had come to lose one shoe. As the search party was again beginning to cross the stepping-stones, a cheerful shout came down from halfway up the rocky path which led up the far bank of the river.

"Hello there! Hiya, Dad! Steve, Jane, Sarah! Hiya! I'm up here!"

Startled eyes turned upward. A relieved Mr. Fern saw his missing son limping down the path. The other children were calling excitedly back across the river. Peter Barr and his twin sister, Anne, always adventurous, jumped recklessly across the stones and ran up the path to meet Roger. Mark called out, "That's all right then, Mr. Fern . . ." His words trailed off, and he gave an odd sort of gasp. "But, gor! Look who's up there with 'im. Look who it is!"

7
Alb'Erratt

When Roger was nine years old, he had broken his left arm one evening at Cubs, in the grounds of his father's school, playing on one of the old logs and slipping on the smooth wood. He was thinking of this episode now, as he sat on a jutting-out stone halfway up the rocky slope from the brook to the fields over which lay his path toward Hilltree Clump. He was remembering the pain in his arm, the dull ache which had spread slowly from arm to shoulder, from shoulder to side, to head, and then had made his legs wobbly until he had felt "like death warmed up," as his father was fond of saying. He was beginning to feel like that a bit now, he thought miserably. His leg was awful. What a mess to be in—miles from any-where—and his leg crippling him. The scratches on his face were feeling sore again too, and the ones on his legs.

He had had no luck when he reached the brook and searched for his shoe, and so he had tried to press on without it. The path had been too steep, too rough for his bad foot, and now here he sat, wondering what on earth to do next, growing cold, ravenously hungry one minute, yet feeling a bit sick the next because of the throbbing pain from his left ankle. What a day he had had—scratched all over in a bramble bath, attacked by a mad dog, chased by the dreaded Alberrutt and the dog again, and now a twisted ankle. What a way to ruin a day that should have been the best they all had ever had. Had the others at the quarry picnic begun wondering where he was yet, Roger asked himself, or were they all still stuffing their selfish selves?

He decided to try to make a crutch or walking stick. There was a birch sapling only a few yards from where he sat. He hobbled, gasping, across to it, but the wood was too springy and would not break. He slumped back to the ground and sat in utter misery, elbows on knees, hands holding up his chin, wondering what to do or to try next. The sun was getting quite low. The afternoon was hurry-ing on. Already the bottom of the little valley was in shadow. He was too low down, sitting on this path, to be able to see across the trees and up the distant fields towards the Grays' Farm. Perhaps he had better try to get higher up this slope and then signal across to the farm. But what with?

He had simply no means of signaling except by yelling and perhaps waving his shirt on the end of a long pole. But he had already tried and failed to break a pole, and his shirt was one of those very useful gray ones that would show up in the distance about as well as a black cat on a coal heap. No, of course, he didn't have his shirt on. He had borrowed Mark's jersey, and that was no good for signaling either, being green. Perhaps everyone ought to wear some garment of that vivid orangey-yellow color that aircraft dinghies were made of, so as to be able to signal on occasions like this. Imagine wearing flamboyant yellow vest and pants. He giggled feverishly.

At that moment, a low and tuneless whistle from up the path to his right made him gasp and turn his head toward the sound. He heard stones clattering as the footsteps came nearer and the whistling grew louder.

"Help, please! I've hurt my leg," Roger shouted, and was thankful to hear the hurried slithering of shoes or boots.

A few seconds later the half-jumping, half-running figure of a man appeared around the corner of the winding path.

"Proper startled me, you did, calling out like that," the man said, "Hurt your leg, 'ave you? Didn't reckon on meeting anyone here. How'd you hurt yourself?"

He bent down, and Roger felt nimble, strong fingers feeling their way down his sock. He gasped as the man gently pulled down the sock and touched the swollen ankle. "Ah, sprained it, I guess. An' where's the shoe? And them scratches—how'd you get them? You look like the wreck o' the 'Esperus."

Roger poured out his story. How many times had he explained about the scratches already? But this time, as before, his relief was so great that he spoke willingly, assured from the man's tone of voice that he would be helped.

The man knelt down by Roger. He took a big red handkerchief out of his jacket pocket and tied it swiftly and expertly, it seemed to Roger, around the swollen ankle. As the man bent down, Roger looked at him and wondered.

He was small, only a few inches taller than Roger himself, and neatly made. He wore an old sports jacket, patched at the elbows and sleeves, and stained flannel trousers. He had no tie on, but a scarf instead. His face was narrow, his ears high on the sides of his head and slightly pointed at the top, giving him a faintly elvish look. How old he was, Roger could not guess. Forty or fifty? His skin was brown and weathered. But what caught Roger's gaze was his hair. It was cropped quite short. It was snowy white. The contrast with the brown of his neck was startling. Roger was caught goggling, and flushed as the man looked up and said, "Yes, queer, isn't it? The war did it. Makes me look hundred years old, I reckon. Don't you worry, though. I'm young enough to see you back to where you wanna go." He grinned and Roger grinned back, glad that the man did not mind mentioning his queer white hair, and feeling, now he had seen that grin, that his worries were over.

"Thanks," he said. "It feels a bit better the way you've

tied it up. Will you really help me? I've got to get to Hilltree Clump."

"What, up the bridle road, t'other side this hill? What for?"

"I suppose it is no good going there now," admitted Roger. "I was supposed to get there by twelve. It's a good bit past that now, I guess. I'm meeting my brother there, so we can go on together to a picnic with our cousins from Bristol."

"Twelve!" The man laughed. "It's nearer three, I shouldn't wonder. Where's this picnic you're all trying to get to, then?"

"At the Pine Tree Quarry" said Roger. "I don't know what the place is really called. We've been coming here for years now, ever since my cousins moved to Bristol. The district's about halfway for us all, so we meet at the little quarry. It's all grassy at the bottom and nice and sheltered, and it's safe to light a fire, and we cook sausages and . . ." He stopped and licked his lips. "I'm absolutely starving. I don't suppose there'll be much grub left, but I'd better try and get there again." He stood up, wobbling as he tried his weak leg on the ground.

"Yes, but where is this little quarry, then?" The man chuckled. "There's dozens of little quarries round here— and a few big 'uns. Which one is your picnic place?"

"It's near the road, about a mile out of Upton, I think, and there's a clump of bushes near one side of it, and two or three big pine trees—or larch or something," Roger said. "I wonder if I can cut across somewhere straight to it."

"If it's where I think you mean, you can't," said the man. "But I reckon if I put you on the right path—we shall 'ave to go back across the brook and down the other side—then you'll be all right."

He turned toward a tree, swiftly took out a worn, one-bladed pocketknife and cut a four-foot length of branch. Expertly he trimmed the thinner end so that it was like a scout's walking stick, but with longer sides to the fork. He handed it to Roger and said, "How's that for a crutch? Try it and see."

"Gosh, thanks." Roger took it, fitted the fork under his armpit, and put the other end on the ground. His companion stooped, nicked the stick an inch or two from the end and took it again. "Bit too long," he said, and quickly carved off the unwanted piece. "There you are. Made to measure." He grinned. "Coming?"

Carefully, using his crutch as much as possible, and taking all the support he could get from the man, Roger managed to get down the slope. He was so intent on not losing his footing again that he noticed nothing ahead of him until the man at his side suddenly said, "Some people down by the brook. Lot of 'em. Kids too, by the sound of 'em. Perhaps it's your brother and cousins come to look for you."

Roger looked eagerly ahead. The trees were too thick, but a few more steps and he could see the twinkling brook below him. Someone in blue jeans was on the middle stepping-stone. It looked like young Peter! A tall man was bending down at the far side of the stream. As he straightened up, Roger recognized his father. He let out

74

an excited yell. "Hello there! Hiya, Dad! Steven, Jane, Sarah! Hiya! I'm up here!"

He saw surprised faces turn up toward him. He hurried, hobbling, down to meet them. He could see Peter and Anne racing, bent nearly double, up the slope. There was Mark too by the stepping-stones, and he was pointing, pointing past Roger to the man who had helped him. Roger heard him cry out in surprise. "Look who's up there with 'im, Mr. Fern. Look who it is! Alb 'Erratt!"

A dozen hands helped Roger down the path to the brook. Everyone seemed eager to help the long-lost and apparently wounded hero. Everyone gasped at his appearance; his wildly scratched face, his tousled hair, his jersey instead of a shirt, his torn and stitched-up coat, his scratched hands and wrists, his tattered trousers, his snagged socks, his muddy and bramble-slashed knees and legs, and his bandaged and shoeless left foot, resplendent in a borrowed red wrapping.

"I don't know," said Stephen in amazement. "He looked bad enough when I left him, just scratched a bit . . ."

"A bit! I like that!" yelled Roger, excited and now so safe.

". . . but look at him now! He looks as thought he's been run over by a couple of cars, trampled by an elephant or two, fallen over a cliff, jumped out of an airplane without a parachute— What a scarecrow!"

"Still," said Sarah, who for one was glad to see that her favorite cousin was safe and sound at last and did not mind showing it. "Still, we've found you. Are you hungry?" she asked, and smiled as she offered him the paper bag she had been carrying. "It's a bit bent, I expect. I had to cram it into my anorak pocket, and Mary's been sitting on me in the car, but I think it's still eatable."

Roger took it, looked inside the bag and crowed, "Sausage pie! Good ol' Sarah! Thanks! Marvelous!" He shoved into his mouth a handful of broken pastry and munched happily.

"Here's your shoe, young Rog," said Mr. Fern. "A bit wet, but you won't notice that, will you? Do you think you can get it on? It might make walking a bit easier."

"I'll try, Dad. Then perhaps I can give this hanky back to Mr. . . . Mr. . . . Where is he?"

Roger looked round. The man who had helped him was a good way behind, holding back, unwilling to join the excited group of searchers. Roger waved and shouted, "Come on, mister. My dad wants to thank you." The man had stopped. He seemed uncertain.

Mark, by Roger's side, said indignantly, "Thank 'im! It's 'im whose dog went for that lamb, Mr. Fern, and tore Roger's coat, and—" The enormity of suggesting thanking a man like that temporarily made him speechless.

"Don't be daft, Mark. He couldn't have. And he's helped me a lot. He tied up my ankle, made me this crutch and—" Roger stopped. He felt he could not properly explain how the man had done more than the things he had mentioned: that he had cheered him up just when his spirits had sunk to their lowest point, that he had appeared on the scene just when another second of loneliness would have made Roger cry with despondency.

"Huh," Mark grunted. "Another minute or two an' we should 'a' found you ourselves."

Roger looked again at the white-haired man. He had come no farther down the path. Roger turned and hobbled back toward him. His father and Dr. Barr followed and then caught him up and steadied him. The man came down toward them. He seemed altogether different from the cheerful, talkative, friendly man he had been when alone with Roger. He dropped his eyes and spoke shyly.

"You'll be all right now then, young 'un," he said gruffly.

"Yes, we'll keep him out of any more silly tricks now," said Mr. Fern. "And I'm very grateful to you. If you'd like your handkerchief back, I'll put mine round his ankle."

"No, keep it—won't matter," Alb 'Erratt said hurriedly and turned. "I got to go now." He strode off quickly up the path and disappeared among the trees.

"Queer chap," said Mr. Fern. "Come on, young Rog. Down to that stone by the brook and let your uncle have a look at that ankle. Queer little chap!"

"Yes," agreed Dr. Barr. He stared thoughtfully up the path where Alb 'Erratt had disappeared, and then bent down and examined his nephew's ankle.

Once he had pronounced it merely sprained and had

helped Roger into his newly found shoe, the plentiful helping hands gathered around Roger and the procession back began. It proved rather difficult to help Roger over the stepping-stones, and both Mary and Peter got a wetting when Peter slipped off one stone, grabbed Mary's arm and pulled her off. He very nearly pulled Roger off too, but—"Not quite," groaned Stephen, as he saw it. "Gosh, if he'd gone into the brook, then—wow!" Luckily the two young Bristolites got no more than wet feet and, as their father said, that was nothing new on a picnic.

And so the eleven of them slowly mounted the sloping fields back to Grays' Farm. Neither Roger nor Mark mentioned Alb 'Erratt again, nor did Roger say anything about the heavy golden coin that jingled between the two half-crowns in his back pocket, or the tiny cube of stone.

8
Meetings and Farewells

There was plenty of talk about Alb 'Erratt in the Grays'
farmhouse kitchen when all of them had crowded in and
Mr. and Mrs. Gray had been flooded with their nephew
Mark's excited descriptions of everything that had happened. Mr. Gray, a big and quiet man, had been glad to
meet Roger and to thank him for his plucky fight with the
dog, but he had to admit that it could hardly have been
Alb 'Erratt's dog, if, as he had told Roger, he had been
away in Cheltenham for the past two days. So whose dog
had it been that had savaged the lamb?

"I heard a man in the woods near the brook," added
Roger, "and he swore at the dog with him, and he called
it Bab."

"Didn't you see him then?" asked Mrs. Gray.

"No," said Roger. He added awkwardly, "Actually I heard the dog coming down the path, and I hid till they'd gone by. I'm sure it was the same dog again. I didn't see it, but the barks sounded the same."

"Oh, well," said Mr. Gray. "I saw old caravans and trucks along the main road, up by the all-night road-house. It was probably one o' them folk out for a stroll to see what he could find to pick up free."

"Well, I'm glad," said Mrs. Gray. "I'm glad it wasn't poor Alb 'Erratt. I know everyone thinks he's strange, and he gets blamed for everything, but I don't think he's anything more than a tiny bit queer in the head and a lot lonely."

"Yes," said Mr. Gray and explained what his wife meant to Mr. Fern and Dr. Barr and the older children (the younger ones were outside with Jim the farmhand, helping to feed the chickens and watching the milking). "Poor Albert, he was blown up in the war. Some bomb or shell went off just as his squad was digging it out. Bomb disposal he was in. He was unconscious for weeks, and he was never the same man again. His hair went pure white and his nerves were all . . . blown to bits, so they said. Never been able to do a job since then, and that's nearly twenty years since. He came back to work on the farm here, but he wasn't any good. All nervous, no control at all, like I said." Mr. Gray sighed. "And like the missis says, he gets blamed for everything round here—poaching, breaking down the walls, setting his dog on the lambs, and the ewes, the lot. Seems we're a bit hard on him, though, at least over this last do this morning."

"Well," said Roger, "he's certainly got white hair, but otherwise you might be talking about a different man. He was nothing like you said. He wasn't nervous. He was jolly kind and as nice as anything."

"Must be the effect you have on people, young Roger," said Dr. Barr, smiling.

"Yes," said Mr. Fern. "Though he went off in a hurry as soon as I went to thank him for helping Roger. Must be the effect *I* have on people!"

Stephen and Sarah and Jane and Roger were by this time becoming rather restless, so Mr. Fern stood up and said good-bye to the Grays. "We must go back and pack up that picnic and get off toward home," he said. He saw the children look disappointed and added, "There may be just time for a game of cricket if we're lucky. Can Mark come?"

This time there were eleven to cram into the old Humber, but no one minded the squash, least of all Roger, who was still luxuriating in the many companions all around him, though he did get one painful knock on his sore left ankle when Tim climbed onto his lap.

"So long," called Mr. Fern to the Grays. We'll bring Mark back when we call in for Roger's bicycle on the way home."

"See you later then," called Mr. Gray. "Nice lot o' folks," he said, when they had gone, and chuckled. "That young Roger! What didn't happen to him! He certainly stood up for Alb 'Erratt and no mistake." He looked up at the sky. "Cricket . . . They'll be lucky! Football, if they had floodlights, but not much light left for cricket now." The sky had suddenly darkened and it was colder. The glorious sunshine of the early spring day was nearly over, and rain and a storm seemed likely. "Ah, cricket," mused Mr. Gray. "They must be eager, as early as this."

Fortunately for the eager cricketers, the two mothers had done all the packing up, ready for a quick getaway, when the search party returned to the picnic quarry with the lost hero. A bright wood fire was flaming on the hearth of stones and a big old blackened kettle was bubbling away softly. Roger was once more joyously welcomed back by his mother and aunt and once more heard the astonished surprise that his appearance seemed to cause in every grown-up he met. His mother took a lot of reassuring that underneath all the scratches and tears and limps and bruises and other people's clothes ("Oh, Mum! It's only Mark's jersey") there was the same Roger Fern she had cheerfully waved to as he set off, neat and tidy and unharmed, on his bike from Dingham railway station.

He sat down next to her in one of the folding metal deck chairs and again told the story of his eventful day while all the others got on with the cricket game in the field above. And while he talked he ate, and ate, and ate. He had already had the last slice of sausage pie, thanks to good old Sarah; now he set about the rest of the picnic. He finished up the sardine sandwiches and the ham sandwiches and the four tomatoes, including the one that Tim and Peter had squashed when they dropped a bottle of pop on the bag of tomatoes when unpacking the food. He cleared up the molasses tart, crumbs and all, and the chocolate sponge cake and the full can of mandarin oranges and the full can of evaporated milk. He drank every last drop of pop, orange squash and lemon squash, and milk and then nibbled up all the remaining biscuits and cheese straws and potato crisps. Finally he tackled the oranges and apples, and when nothing, quite nothing was left of all the picnic food that he could see, he sat back in his deck chair and sighed in satisfaction. "I think it was almost worth all the scratches and bumps and this ankle, Mum, to have a nice peaceful feed like that. I mean, picnics are all right, but when all the others are here you have a job getting your fair share of the grub, don't you?"

In the meadow from which the little quarry had been scooped, like a huge spoonful of rocks and soil out of a smooth dishful of grassland, the cricket game at last came regretfully to an end as the light grew dimmer and dimmer, not so much from evening drawing on as from ugly black clouds appearing from the west. The equipment was collected, and everyone trooped down the path to the quarry's grassy floor, where the fire flamed invitingly and the kettle steamed, and Mrs. Fern and Mrs. Barr had the teacups laid out ready.

"Lucky I always keep the tea food separate in the car and don't get it out till we want it," said Mrs. Fern, "or Roger would have finished the lot. Having a bramble bath must be good for the appetite, eh, Rog?"

Roger agreed that something had happened that day to make him feel hungry, and though it was less than half an hour since he had finished his belated picnic dinner, he joined in the tea feast energetically enough. The fresh air everyone had been breathing all day had sharpened their appetites, and once more every dish, paper bag, and bottle was emptied.

Dr. Barr said he thought they had perhaps better get a move on, as the clouds were coming up very darkly. Mr. Fern and Stephen dampened out the fire with the tea dregs and then put flat stones on top of the embers and ashes and made sure it was quite safe.

Peter Barr brought the last plastic can of water from the car and that was tipped onto the fireplace, where it hissed and brought up fountains of steam and white wood-ash.

Stephen got on his bike when he had said good-byes all around. "I'll meet you at Grays' Farm, then. Cheerio, Jane and Sarah. We've had a good day, haven't we?"

His uncle called out, "Are you sure *you* won't get lost this time?"

Stephen grinned and pedaled off through the gateway and onto the road. "Cheerio!" he shouted and was gone.

The big old groundsheet was rolled up after all the crumbs had been shaken off it. The bags and bottles and cans and all the picnic paraphernalia were packed away and carried to the two cars by the eight remaining children, for Mark was joining in everything as though he were one of the family now. The deck chairs were folded up and stacked on the roof racks. "Good thing these are all alloy and plastic. Won't matter if they do get wet," said Dr. Barr. He and Mr. Fern took a final look around the now empty little quarry to check whether anything had been left behind and strolled back to the cars.

Mrs. Fern said to her brother and all the Barrs, "Sorry we've messed the day up so much. Poor old Roger's plans . . ." She was quickly interrupted.

"Don't be daft, my dear," insisted Mrs. Barr. "That made the day. We shan't forget last April Fools' Day, and we certainly shan't forget today either. Up the Ferns! Cheerio!"

"Cheerio. See you at Whitsun perhaps?"—and the Barrs were gone. The Ferns and Mark dashed into the car as splatters of rain fell coldly, and drove back to Grays' farm. Stephen, they saw, was inside the house, waiting for them.

"Come on inside," shouted Mr. Gray, and they all ran through the rain thankfully into the warmth of the farmhouse, where Mrs. Fern met the Grays and thanked Mrs. Gray for being so kind to Roger.

"Better leave your bike where it is, young man," said Mr. Gray to Roger. "You'll never ride all that way with your bad foot, and this rain'd soak you 'fore you got to the end of the lane."

"Yes, and yours too," said Mrs. Gray to Stephen. "You don't want to get drenched and then have to sit in the car for hours on end in wet clothes. You can both leave your bikes in our barn. Then Jeff'll take 'em to the station one day later in the week and send them on to you, won't you, Jeff?",

"Sure. Glad to," said Mr. Gray.

"Fine," agreed Stephen and Roger, and Mrs. Fern smiled her thanks.

"Yes, I'm sure I shall feel happier if these two are

safely in the car with us," she said, "especially now it's come on like this." As she spoke, the rain lashed against the windowpanes and rattled the door latch. "We've got a wet drive to Cambridge ahead of us."

The Ferns had farther to go than the Barrs, and the boys knew that the best way to pass the time was to try to sleep, especially as it was getting too dark, and they were too tired to play pub cricket or any of the car number-plate games they usually played on journeys in daylight. But Roger in the back seat was not dozing very comfortably. He wriggled and moved this way and that, being careful not to disturb Stephen, who was always very snappy when knocked or nudged in his car sleeps. Then he realized what it was making him so uncomfortable. It was the things in his back trouser pocket. Very cautiously he eased himself upright, put his hand into his pocket and drew out the four objects. Lovingly he fondled them in the dark, the two exactly similar coins, which were the half-crowns Mrs. Gray had given him for a new cycle pump, the other heavier coin, not exactly circular, his fingers told him, and the tiny cube of stone. He gently put them all into his jacket pocket, kept his hand in with them, and settled back in the car seat. What a day it had been . . . What a day . . . What a day . . .

And as the car sped on smoothly eastwards, Roger happily dozed off, his fingers tightly clutching the heavy coin marked on one side *NERO* and on the other *ROMA.*

9
Seven Long Weeks

What always amazed Roger afterwards was how completely he kept the secret. There was, too, the queer feeling when he woke up late on the Tuesday morning following the picnic and realized that he was a hundred miles away from the little grassy quarry and the river and the birch tree half-uprooted and Alb 'Erratt and the Grays and Mark, the queer feeling that it had all been a dream. He needed to get out of bed, forgetting his twisted ankle and getting a reminding twinge as he jumped out recklessly, and to feel yet again in his old jacket pocket and to finger the coin and the stone cube. They were real enough. He reluctantly reached out his hand to put the two back into his jacket and then, with a sigh of relief as he thought about it, remembered that his mother would be sure to take the jacket downstairs to mend the tear which Mrs. Gray had roughly tacked up for him after the dog had ripped it. He knew his mother's cleanly habit of turning out all jacket pockets on such occasions, with the idea that while she had her mending things out she might as well see that the pockets were whole and that the fluff and toffee papers were emptied out. She would be sure to find the coin and the stone if he left them in the coat pocket. Roger thought for a moment and then hobbled over and hid them both in the cardboard box which contained his electric train controller. No one would ever look there.

For nearly a week everything seemed to combine to drive the memories of the picnic and his adventures far back into the past and almost out of mind. This week was the final week of the school Easter holidays, and there was a lot to be done, both in the garden of the old cottage where the Ferns were living temporarily and in the garden of their new house, which was about to be built half a mile farther along the village. Mr. and Mrs. Fern firmly believed that the new house would be ready to move into by the next Christmas and were determined that the garden should be well advanced so as to give a good show the following spring. So while Mr. Fern, Stephen, and Tim were setting potatoes in the cottage garden, Mrs. Fern would take Roger along to the new garden to do some cleaning up of the ground, which had lain fallow for years and so was infested with stinging nettles, briars, horseradish, and couch grass. The hedges needed cutting too, and many weary arm-aching hours both Stephen and Roger spent, slashing fiercely with a billhook at the long thorny growths that twined and bent out of so many patches of hedge. There was only one slasher, as they called the hook, so they had to do fifteen-minute stints each. Roger, one day near the end of the holiday week, stopped slashing before his time was up.

"Come on, Steve," he called. "You have to go now. I'm fed up with it."

"Five more minutes at least," said Stephen. "Do your share."

"Oh, I'm fed up. The blooming brambles are every-where. Can't you burn 'em out of the hedge, Dad? It'd save a lot of work."

Mr. Fern straightened from where he was digging up horseradish roots on a patch of ground planned to be the new lawn. "No, sorry, Rog. You'll have to keep on slashing at least a bit longer."

"I know, Rog," said Stephen, chuckling. "Think of those briars you fell in by the gate at that prehistoric earthworm. Then you'll enjoy slashing these."

It worked miracles. Roger renewed his attack on the brambles, wielding the slasher like a two-handed sword. He began growling, "Take that! And that! That one's for the scratch across my face! That's for my arm! That's for my sore seat! My sore knees! Take that, you rotten thorns! Take that!"

He soon finished his full fifteen minutes of attack, handed over to Stephen, and said, "Thanks, Steve. Good

idea. I enjoyed that. Got back at the brambles. Phew!"
He sat down on a plum tree stump and said to his father,
"Dad, are my scratches nearly better?"

"Yes," said Mr. Fern. "All those I can see. How
about the hidden ones?"

"They're O.K. I can sit down better now. And my
ankle's fine. Dad, when are we going down to the
quarry again for another picnic?"

"Picnic?" said Mr. Fern. He mopped the sweat from
his brow. The day was warm and sultry for April.
"I don' know. Not until the Whitsun holiday, I guess
—at least, if you mean to meet the Bristolites there
again."

"When's Whitsun, Dad?" Roger asked.

"Seven weeks after Easter."

"Seven weeks! Gosh, that's years!"

"Six weeks now. One week's nearly gone," said
Stephen.

"Oh, lor! I want to go back and see Mark before
then," insisted Roger.

"Can't be done. Sorry. Six weeks isn't very long.
It'll soon pass . . . that is if we really do go down there
again then," said Mr. Fern.

"Oh yes, we must. Mustn't we, Steve?" Roger felt
he had to make it quite clear.

"It'd be all right," Stephen said, without any particular
keenness in his voice.

"We practically promised Mrs. Gray and Mark," said
Roger.

"Yes, well, we probably shall go. No need to go on

about it. Why are you so keen, Rog? Want to have another bramble bath?"

"No fear! I just feel like seeing Mark again . . . and," he added, "I didn't get a game of cricket last time. I was crippled, remember? I had to sit watching."

"You had to sit eating!" His father smiled.

"Well, anyway, I missed the cricket game."

And so it was left, half-settled in Roger's mind that they would all be going to the quarry or to Grays' Farm again in the Whitsun holidays, a long, long, six weeks ahead.

On the Saturday before the end of the holidays, the parcel containing the shirt came from Mrs. Gray, with a little note inside saying that she and Mr. Gray hoped Roger had gotten over his scratches and sprained ankle. She also said that the weather had been terrible since the day all the Ferns and Barrs had been there. It had rained and rained nearly all the time and all the fields were soaking. Roger at once wrote back.

> *Dale Farm Cottage*
> *Little Stinton*
> *Near Cambridge*
> *April 15th*

Dear Mrs. Gray,

Thank you very much for the shirt, which came today. It was nice of you to wash it, though Mum says you shouldn't have. Will you ask Mark if he wants me to send his jersey back to him, or will it do when we come next time? I don't know when

that will be because Dad says there's so much to
do in the garden here and only a day or two left
this holiday. So it will most likely be Whitsun.
My ankle is better now and so are the scratches.
Thank you for the shirt.

Roger Fern
P.S. I hope that dog hasn't gone for any more
lambs, and I hope the bad weather you've had
didn't blow any more trees down.

When his mother read this—she still liked to check
that her sons had fully done their duty in thanking all
relations and friends for presents and so on—she said,
"What's this about trees blowing down, Roger?"

"Oh, I mean, well . . . the trees look jolly nice down
by that brook . . . and I hope none of them have been
blown down. Mrs. Gray said they'd been having storms
these last few days since we came home."

"Oh, I see," said Mrs. Fern, rather puzzled that Roger
should suddenly show concern for some trees a hundred
miles away. Boys were queer things. She shrugged
and forgot it. Roger realized how nearly he had given
the game away and hurriedly licked the envelope and
stuck it down. He ran out to mail the letter, still wondering whether the storms down at the Grays' farm had done
any damage to the lovely trees in the woods by the river,
especially the "rocket" birch. That was what Roger had
decided to name the half-toppled-over tree under whose
roots he had hidden from the dog and found the coin.
Six more weeks, he thought miserably, as he pushed the
letter into the wall-box mouth, six more weeks in which

to worry and wonder if that lovely glade would stay the same and wait for him to go and search under the tree root. Six more weeks.

But even six long slow weeks come to an end. The boy's bicycles soon returned from Grays' Farm, so some rides were possible. Then, too, swimming began in the new pool at Mr. Fern's school, though until the middle of May the water was chilly. Roger borrowed books about coins from the library in Cambridge but could find little to help him understand his rocket-birch find. And then one morning at twenty to eight the postman walked by the cottage window and pushed a letter under the door. Tim, who had just put his face up for his mother to smell the soap to prove he had washed, called, "I'll get it, Mummy," and scurried out. He carried the letter slowly back, trying to see whose it was. In triumph he read out, "Roger Fern. It's for you, Roger. Can I open it?"

Roger looked at the postmark and nearly choked with excitement. "It's from Mark, I bet," he said. "Yes, O.K., Tim. Here's the knife. Careful. Be quick. It's nearly time for the bus." He crammed the last of his toast into his mouth and took the letter from Tim. "Oh, great!" he breathed, and turned to the table. "Dad, Mum, it's from Mark. Can I go and stay with him at Whitsun? He says his mum'd love to have me and Stephen. They think there's a bus we could go on."

The school bus, everyone knew, would wait for nothing, so there was no time to go into the details of Mark's suggestion. Roger and Stephen went off to school in some excitement at the thought of what Whitsun could now mean. Roger felt all the thrills flooding back at the thought of seeing "Narnia" and the rocket birch again. Should he tell Stephen? And Stephen was pleased at the idea of some days in the Cotswolds, because he wanted to try some oil painting. The brief glimpse of that lovely little river, and the waterfall he had heard but not seen . . . . Yes, it would be great to go down there again.

At home later that evening the times were worked out and everything was arranged to Roger's and Stephen's satisfaction. But not to Tim's. He was most upset to hear that he would be left behind and had a fit of tantrums until Mrs. Fern suggested that it would be a good idea for the three of them to go down by car and fetch Roger and Stephen back, at the end of Whit week.

"Oh, Daddy," said Tim, with eyes wide. "Can we have a day off school just for that?"

"It'll be the holidays, Tim. Whit week. We shall all have a week's holiday." Mr. Fern smiled.

"And I can stay up late then?" insisted Tim. That was agreed, though everyone knew that Tim always slept soundly in the car when coming back from any distance.

Roger wrote back to Mark saying that he and Stephen were looking forward to going, and thanking him for the invitation. Roger looked up the dates on the calendar. "Gosh," he groaned. "It's four weeks still to go. Nearly five. Roll on, Whitsun, eh, Steve? Come, on Tim, give a shout. All together—*Roll on, Whitsun!*"

Mr. and Mrs. Fern smiled and thought the same thought themselves. That very day the foundations of

94

their new house had been started and by Whitsun they hoped to see great progress. So, roll on, Whitsun, they silently agreed.

When at last it was Whit Tuesday morning, the day for the bus ride down to the Cotswolds, Roger felt a qualm of disappointment as he thought how little he had found out about Roman coins in that seven weeks. He was really no nearer. Perhaps he had been wrong in trying to do it all by himself. Perhaps he ought to have told Stephen or his father. Too late now, he thought, packing his little suitcase.

Stephen too had packed by the time Roger got downstairs. He was taking a box of oil paints and a roll of special paper. There was no room for a decent drawing-board. Then, with kisses on their cheeks from Mrs. Fern, they got into the car with Tim and Mr. Fern. Mr. Fern maneuvered carefully around the narrow paths by the cottage onto the main farmhouse driveway, and they were away, Tim's hand fluttering farewells to his mother out of the back window.

At Cambridge bus station they were seen onto the morning bus to Cheltenham and reminded to get off at Bourton.

"See you on Saturday," called Tim and Mr. Fern, and then the bus rolled away and began its long journey to the southwest. As he walked with Tim back to the parking lot, Mr. Fern said, "I wonder what they'll get up to this time, Tim. What do you think?"

"Lots o' things, I expect," said Tim. "Lots of things, Daddy."

10

Left Hand Wood

The bus rolled into Bourton almost exactly on time, at two-forty, and the boys had been up to nothing so far, except that Stephen, who was fond of sweets, had nearly missed the bus while dashing out to a shop near where the bus stopped at Chipping Norton. They were both very thankful to get off and into the fresh May air of the little Cotswold town as they climbed down the bus steps and said, "Cheerio," to the conductor.

They had hardly time to put their cases down on the ground and look around before a grinning Mark ran up and called out delightedly, "'Ello! Got 'ere all right, then? Come on. Dad's over there." He led them across the street to where a Land Rover was waiting.

"Here they are, Dad," Mark said, and Roger and Stephen were introduced to Mr. Burrows. He was short, about five feet five, but very broad and strong looking. His face was as brown as a nut and his eyes were the clearest blue. He held out a big strong hand. "Hello," he said and smiled at Roger. "So you're the one who had all the fun last Easter."

"I don't know about fun," said Roger. Mark put the suitcases in the back of the Land Rover and they all four squashed into the front cab seat. "I didn't enjoy the scratches or the sprained ankle, or the do with the dog, but all the rest of the day was fine."

"Uncle Jeff shot that ol' dog a few days arter you'd gone," said Mark with satisfaction, as they drove off and out of the town. "Caught it going at some more lambs and shot it. You were right. It weren't Alb 'Erratt's. Got no collar on or anything, so might 'ave been anybody's."

"I'm glad it wasn't Alb 'Erratt's," Roger said. He spoke the name with hesitation. It still held some alarm and a lot of mystery for him. He had Alb 'Erratt's red handkerchief in his suitcase, washed and ironed and all ready to hand back if he could find him again.

Mark's mother had the table spread with scones and bread-and-jam and boiled eggs and buns, when they arrived. They felt completely at ease. Mark's parents seemed really glad to see them, and soon Roger and Stephen were sitting back in the comfortable wooden farm-kitchen chairs, feeling rather dozy after their long bus ride and such a satisfying tea.

The Burrows' farm stood at the end of a mile-long

lane leading off the main road. It was similarly placed to the Grays' farm, which was the same distance off the same road but a mile farther south. Like the Grays' farmhouse, too, the Burrows' house was on the side of the little valley, but higher up the stream.

One branch of the stream had its source in a spring only a few yards down the woods past the sloping home field of Burrows' Farm. The woods which followed the stream stopped fifty yards away from the farm buildings, and from the bedroom they had been given, Stephen and Roger could see clear to the west and south through the two windows, one in each wall. To the west rose the rolling uplands, which ended in the flat ground taken over as an airfield. The huge black hangers could just be seen, crouching in the far distance. To the right of these there was a nearer, curious long mound, no more than a mile away. To the south, through the window by the bed which Roger claimed as soon as he saw the view, there stretched the long fingers of massed trees. From here, high up and looking along instead of across the strips of woodland, a clearer idea could be had of the layout of the trees and hills and brooks.

It all looked much more thrilling even than last Easter, thought Roger. And how green everywhere was. He had not realized how bare the trees had been before. Now in late May the trees were in full leaf and the landscape was transformed. He longed to hurry down into the woods and see for himself how it all looked close up. Green, green everywhere. Every field was green, every tree had fluttering full leaves. Roger hurriedly pushed all of the clothes out of his suitcase into the drawers and cupboards by his bed and said impatiently to Stephen, who was sitting on the window seat, looking out, "Come on, Steve. Let's get outside. It's not dark for ages yet. We can have a super look through the woods before then. Come on."

Stephen took out his sketch pad and map. He suggested they both should change into their old jeans if they were going to mess about in the woods. They both changed, and then hurried downstairs.

"It's a great bedroom. Thank you, Mrs. Burrows," said Roger enthusiastically. Mark's mother was doing her ironing and she said, "Good, glad you like it. Got a nice view."

"And thanks for the tea. Though it's made me sleepy," said Stephen.

"Can we go out and look around the fields and woods now?" said Roger.

"Course you can," said Mark. He had been helping fold up the handkerchiefs ready for ironing, but gladly took this chance to escape out of doors to more manly occupations.

"Now go careful, all of you," called out Mrs. Burrows. She came to the door with them and said, "No more scratches or broken ankles, any of you. I heard all about the last time."

"Oh, Mum," complained Mark. "Don't fuss." He called out over his shoulder as they hurried down the slabbed garden path toward the stile, "Cheerio, Mum."

At the stile Stephen stopped and said, "I'd like to make

sure I know where I am on the map. Look." He spread his new one-inch Ordnance Survey map out on his knee as he sat on the top of the stile, and pointed. "Look, it shows your farm, Mark. There . . . See, Roger? If we split up at all, we'd better have some idea of where places are, so we can arrange to meet and so on. If I draw these woods roughly on my sketch pad and we each have a copy with certain spots marked . . ."

He swiftly drew a simplified version of the woodlands shown green on the map. Then he drew in the lines standing for the streams which flowed through the woods. Next he marked the farm.

Roger, watching him intently, said suddenly, "They look a bit like fingers." The other two looked. "Like bones of fingers at least," said Roger.

He placed his hand on the pad where Stephen had sketched the copy of the map. It was his left hand, palm upward.

"Look." He pointed with his right hand to the fingers of woodland. "Thumb, first finger, middle finger—with the farm at the top, third finger—with its top joint separate, and little finger." He stopped. There were two more stretches of woods below the little finger.

"You're right, Rog," said Mark admiringly. "It's just like a bony hand."

"Yes," admitted Stephen. "It is. I'd never have seen it if you hadn't said so, Rog, but now I can't see any other shape but a hand. And this bit can be the wrist," he said, pointing to the first unnamed part of wood.

"And that's the bracelet," said Mark triumphantly. He

looked anxiously at the others and was thrilled when he saw they approved.

Stephen penciled in the names above the fingers of woodland. Then he quickly copied the sketch twice more. All three looked at their rough maps.

Roger said, "Now, are we going to keep together or explore separately?"

Stephen said, "Mark knows the place thoroughly, I should guess. Let him take us and show us everything."

"Will you, Mark?" asked Roger. There was nothing he wanted to do more than rush off through the woods by himself until he could find his own special rocket birch and look underneath its roots, but he saw the sense in what Stephen said about exploring together and could think of nothing to say against the suggestion. He did ask one thing though.

"Mark, whereabouts on this map is the place where we crossed the river last Easter—the Stones, as you call 'em?"

Mark looked, puzzled a moment, and then said, "There." He pointed to the gap in between the third finger's two joints. "That's Uncle Jeff's farm, and there's the Stones."

The Stones, Roger saw, would be in the crack between the third and little fingers. He was satisfied. "Come on, let's go."

The three boys trotted across the meadow, which sloped gently down toward the edge of the middle finger of woodland. Roger saw that most of the trees were oaks. There was a barbed wire fence at the edge. From some

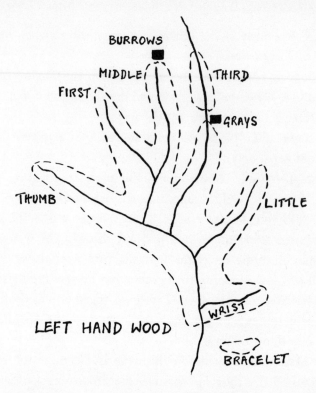

BURROWS

MIDDLE   THIRD

FIRST

GRAYS

THUMB

LITTLE

WRIST

LEFT HAND WOOD

BRACELET

of the barbs hung fluffy balls of pale brown wool. Mark collected all he could find as they walked along the fence, looking for a path into the woods.

"What do you want that for?" said Stephen.

"It's jolly good to put up the toes of your boots if they're too big," said Mark. "Dad allus makes me 'ave my boots nice and big so I don't grow out of 'em too quick. So I collect these wools to put up the toes till they fit me." He cocked his leg over the bottom strand of wire and crawled carefully through. "Mind your breeches. An' your legs, Roger. Remember what my mum said about scratches."

"Oh, shut up," growled Roger. "I'm fed up with being teased about those scratches, especially as it was all Steve's fault. He pushed me off that old gate—as good as."

Mark couldn't tell whether Roger was really cross or not. He decided he would stop joking about the bramble bath. He did not know Roger well enough yet to tell when he was joking or serious.

All six legs managed the fence successfully, and they plunged into the little wood. The ground sloped steeply now, and trickling water was not far ahead of them. The smell of earth, leaves, trees, and flowers was gorgeous. Roger stood still and breathed deeply. "Great," he said. "Just great. You're a lucky chap to live near a place like this, Mark."

"Coo, this en't anything," said Mark. "You wait till you see farther in. It's really pretty in there . . . Well," he added awkwardly, "not pretty, like picture postcards . . . you know?"

They thought they did. Roger looked around happily. Here he was at last, in the same woods as his rocket tree. It had all come true at last.

Stephen looked around too. He was thinking of the colors and how hard it was going to be to get them right when he painted. He could see hundreds of different greens—the yellowy green of the ferns, another green altogether of the yellow nettles, the quite different green of the red campion leaves, yet another green of the blue-bell swords—all these before he took his eyes off the ground and looked at the trees and their greens. That ivy, for instance, growing over a broken birch stump, was dull green near the ground, shiny, different green higher up, different again at the shoot tips. He sighed, both in pleasure at the profusion of colors and shades all around him and in dissatisfaction with the pictures he would paint, knowing that he could never convey all that this beauty meant to him.

"Who do these woods belong to, Mark?" he said, and began walking on down the slope.

"My dad and my aunt and uncle Gray," said Mark. "Both sides of the river, and up the hill t'other side a good bit. There's two farms joined together now and my dad and my uncle work 'em together."

"You lucky fellow," said Roger in admiration. "All this land and these marvelous trees! It's just about the best bit of England there is!"

Mark grinned with pleasure. "'Ten't bad, is it? Come on down and look at the spring." He led the way by a faint, hardly noticeable track. Clearly no one else ever came this way.

Roger, following third in the Indian file, felt a thrill of pure exploring-unknown-territory excitement shiver through him. Bluebells, ferns, and other wild flowers grew nearly as high as his waist. Hazel, holly, and hawthorn bushes tangled across the track, and the boys made a detour. Here and there a dead branch or a whole tree stood gaunt, gray, and bare amid all the profusion of green and life, or lay curled and twisted among the thick grasses and wild plants, causing them to trip and stumble until they became used to the hazards that lay hidden in the dense growth about their feet or dangled from the hanging branches by their heads.

Puffing and panting and feeling hot, though glad of their jeans, the two Fern boys followed Mark until they came to a little grassy clearing. In the middle of the green floor there was a tiny brown hillside, as though the ground had slipped downward a yard. From the side of the exposed soil came bubbling a bright little stream, twinkling and laughing as it ran away down the narrow gorge among the grass and buttercups of the glade. Roger and Stephen gazed entranced at the spring. It was as though a beautifully exact tunnel had been dug out of the tiny hillside for a model railway. But instead of rails and a train, out ran a smooth stream of water which chuckled and tinkled as soon as it reached the daylight. For the first few yards the spring ran over waving grass; then its course narrowed, and it quickened its flow into a little sandy and stony valley it had eaten into the soil. Six or seven yards from its source it disappeared into the thickets and the trees. Its bubbling voice could be heard as it hurried along over the stones of its lower course.

Stephen got out his sketch pad. "I'm going to mark in this spring," he said. "This is a super place." He sat down on the springy turf and swiftly sketched in the spring. "Middle finger, top joint," he said and held out his left hand again. He tapped the finger he had mentioned. "We can call this place just that, can't we? Nobody else would know what we meant, but we'd understand. Hey!" he added, as a fresh thought struck him. "I know what we can call all this wood. You're sure it hasn't got a proper name, Mark?"

"No, just 'the woods,' I reckon," said Mark. "I en't ever heard a name 'part from that—just 'the woods'."

"O.K.," said Stephen. "Then we'll call it Left Hand Wood. And we use the fingers for describing where to meet and so on. Right?"

"Yes, I like that," said Roger. He was dangling his fingers in the tiny stream and feeling the delicious coldness as it trickled past him. "Left Hand Wood. Good name, isn't it, Mark? Left Hand Wood . . . Great!"

11
Middle Finger and Wrist

When the three explorers—or, perhaps, two explorers and their guide—returned to camp that evening the sun was just setting in a dazzling pattern of pink-dappled clouds and turquoise-blue sky. They were all tired, their jeans muddy, and hands and faces dirty, but they were all deliciously, thrillingly happy.

For nearly four hours they had tracked the little stream down the whole of the Middle Finger of Left Hand Wood. They had covered only a mile each way in that time, but so magical was this strip of woods that they had gone very thoroughly and lingeringly, missing no more than a few yards here and there where the thickets over the stream were too dense to penetrate. They had watched the stream grow wider, deeper, and stronger until it was more than they could safely jump. They had found many other tiny springlets joining it until it joined the main stream, which Mark told them flowed down the full length of the Thumb. There they had reluctantly turned and headed home. At each place where a streamlet joined another, or the belt of woodland narrowed, or they came across anything that seemed noteworthy, Stephen had stopped and sketched the detail into his map. The Middle Finger, from the spring to where it joined the main river, was already thickly dotted with his drawings and notes.

Roger and Mark had found fine, long, straight hazel branches in some thickets near the joining of the streams and had had a grand game of spear throwing on the way back. Each boy had a good penknife, and a pointed hazel stick four or five feet long makes a beautiful throwing spear. Mark also cut himself half a dozen other, shorter hazel sticks about a yard long. He wouldn't tell Roger what they were for. "Wait an' see," was all he would say, and he grinned at Roger.

All their spears and sticks were hidden, cached, in a dense holly bush growing at the very tip of the Middle Finger, just inside the barbed wire fence. Mark made quite sure they were all invisible before he carefully edged himself through the double wire and into the field beyond. Then up the slope back to the farmyard stile they trudged. Lights were glowing in the farmhouse. As they watched, they saw someone pull the curtains across in one room of the house. Before they climbed the stile, Stephen took one last look at the superb riot of pink and orange and turquoise and blue that flamed in the sky to the west.

"Had a good day, Rog?" he asked.

"Great, just great," said Rog. "Thanks for inviting us, Mark. We're going to have a super time here." At last they reached the stile and the farmhouse garden.

"Super time . . . and suppertime," said Stephen, grinning, as they all made their way into the kitchen. "Lovely smell, Mrs. Burrows. Beautiful."

The three boys sniffed the appetizing smell of oven cooking. They suddenly remembered that tea had been early and that now it was late. Outside the light had gone. The mild May evening had crept down, with bats hunting around the old farmhouse chimneys, and wide-eyed owls swooping down on the field mice which crept out of Left Hand Wood. But inside the kitchen there was light and warmth and, after a quick scrubbing of hands and changing of muddy jeans and shoes, hot Cornish pasties, with thick gravy streaming down over domes of mashed potatoes.

"You had your teas a bit early, and you've had a good bit of our fresh air all evening, so I guessed you'd be hungry." Mrs. Burrows smiled, and Mr. Burrows crinkled his paper over and over to find the cricket scores. "We don't always have cooked supper as late as this, but your first day here's special, isn't it?"

"Mm, it is, Mrs. Burrows," agreed Roger.

"Some pudding now?" said Mark's mother later, when pasties had been dealt with.

"Just a bit, please."

"You too, Stephen?"

"Please—not too much."

"Australians are wiping the floor with Oxford, I see," said Mr. Burrows. "Got a good team again. Always have though. I reckon it's all that sunshine."

"Dad took us to see them playing Cambridge last week," said Roger, sadly saying no to Mrs. Burrow's offer of more pudding. "They wiped the floor with Cambridge too. Three centuries in their first innings. They only needed to bat once—and the way they hit the ball . . . Cor!"

Their long bus journey, then hours of rambling through woods and thickets, and then this huge meal and the kitchen warmth combined to bring on the yawns suddenly for Roger and Stephen. Willingly they went to bed, though it was not long after nine o'clock. Mark called good night to them and added, "Hope it's another fine day tomorrow. Lot more fingers to explore."

"Good night Mark," Stephen called sleepily. He reached up from his bed and pulled the curtains back. There were stars glittering against the velvety blue-black of the sky. The bright curving lines of the stars in the sickle of the Lion's Head was clear and sparkling. Farther to the northwest the Big Dipper stood up on end. Far away, what sounded like an airplane engine roared, faded, and roared again. Stephen remembered what Mr. Burrows said as they came up to bed.

"Hope you sleep well, boys. Don't take any notice o' me early in the morning. That'll be early milking.

Hope the airplanes don't keep you awake. They'll prob- ably be flying tonight from the camp up on the hill. Don't worry about 'em. They're noisy but they're harmless. Not like some o' them nights in the war."

Dreamily Stephen wondered what had happened on those wartime nights. . . . Less than a minute after pulling the curtains he was asleep.

Roger heard the heavy breathing of his sleeping brother. He too had pulled back the curtains once they had undressed and put out the lights. Now he knelt on the bed and stared out of the open window. The dark countryside lay all around the farm. As his eyes got used to the darkness, Roger could just see the difference be- tween inky-black sky and coal-black ground. The stars were clear, and silently across them twinkled moving red, green, and flashing white lights, followed seconds later by the rolling sound of the distant airplane.

Roger watched the circling lights and sighed. He still had not made up his mind, though he had thought and thought all day about the problem. He had had a fine, long exploration through the woods, but all the time he had been longing to rush down to where his rocket tree was waiting and to search under the roots. It was weeks now since he had found the coin. Someone else might have been and spotted it. What about the storms? Some other trees might have been blown down. It was terrible having to keep a secret like this.

The circling plane swept out of sight behind the hill, another roared up from the airfield, and Roger slipped into bed. As he drifted into sleep, he resolved that in the morning he would tell Stephen and Mark, and then they could all go and see whatever lay waiting under the birch tree roots. Maybe they would meet Alb 'Erratt again.

Next morning by half past ten, after a late sleep, the three boys again crossed the stile and trotted down the field toward the top joint of Middle Finger. The weather looked settled, and Mrs. Burrows had allowed them to take the day's food with them so that they need not go back for dinner. Stephen had in his duffle bag a cut loaf, a packet of butter, knives and spoons, a can of corned beef, a box of cheeses, and his sketch pad. In a haversack made out of his father's old Air Force gas mask holder, Roger was carrying a can of pineapple and a can of evaporated milk. At the very bottom also was his matchbox and its precious contents and a pocket flashlight. Mark's load, also in an old duffle bag, included a packet of crackers, a can of baked beans, some plastic plates and a special folding picnic can opener, and three plastic cups. He had taken the can of beans without his mother knowing. He knew she hated them to be eaten cold, but he loved them that way and so, he hoped, would Stephen and Roger. In his right jacket pocket, as well as his penknife, he had two packets of fizzy drink tablets. Added one at a time to a cup of water, they fizzed marvelously and made a passable lemon- or orange-flavored drink. He had a packet of each flavor. Recently he had begun sucking them. He had found them deliciously sharp and tingling, but he had to swallow a lot, and quickly, or else the bubbles overflowed down his chin. In his left pocket he had half a ball of strong string, the white, smooth sort, not the brown, hairy, weak sort.

The oak trees were rustling welcomingly as they turned off the well-worn footpath that led down outside the woods on its way to Grays' Farm. They had only a few yards to go to reach the holly bush where their weapon cache was. Mark wriggled under the bottom strand of barbed wire, safely into the Top Joint, and carefully pulled out the three spears and the handful of shorter hazel wands he had left with them. All three boys were wearing jeans and windbreaker jackets and wellington boots, all fairly old things, so Roger and Stephen willingly flung themselves down onto the turf and wriggled under the wire after Mark, who handed out the spears. Then they followed the previous day's trail to the spring. It was there that Roger decided he must share his secret or burst. But first there was something else.

"Hang on, you two," he called as Mark, he thought, seemed about to press on farther down the little stream. "I've got something to show you."

"We'd better get on, Rog," said Stephen. "Only three days to explore all of Left Hand Wood, you know. Is it important?"

"Yes, it is. Hang on." Roger was struggling to push his hand down inside the old khaki gas mask holder's narrow pocket. After a moment's finger-wriggling around the bottom of the bag he pulled out a folded, vivid-red handkerchief. "Alb 'Erratt's," he said. "You know—he tied it around my ankle. I want to take it back to him."

"We don't know where he'll be," objected Stephen.

"You do, don't you, Mark?" insisted Roger.

"Well, yes. But . . . you don' wanna worry 'bout that ol' hanky. 'Ten't worth going all that way for. Let me give it to Uncle Jeff. 'E works for 'im a bit. 'E'll give it over next time 'e sees 'im."

Roger smiled at the confusion of 'es and 'ims in Mark's speech. But he understood perfectly well. "No," he said awkwardly. "I want to give it back myself. I didn't ever thank him properly for helping me. Show us where he lives, Mark. Show us on the maps."

So Mark described the old cabin where Alb 'Erratt lived. It was an old building that had once been used as a quarry storehouse, but when the quarry had been closed down years before, Alb 'Erratt had found the loneliness of the place to his liking and had settled there. The cabin stood in the narrow belt of trees now called the Wrist of Left Hand Wood. All three of the boys sketched in the position on their sketch maps of the whole woods, which they each kept in their pockets.

"That's two miles from here, Rog," complained Stephen. "It'd take all day to get there and back, and we'd have no time left for any real exploring."

"I want to go," said Roger, stubbornly. "If I go now and hurry, I could be back in about two hours. You say where we'll meet and I'll be there . . ."—he looked at his watch, which he had been careful to bring with him this time—". . . about three o'clock."

"Oh, no! You don't mean you're going off on your own again, not after last time!" Stephen said in a shocked voice.

"You've been saying how useful the maps would be for planning where to meet and that sort of thing. Now's our chance to try it out." Roger sounded determined. "Go on, say where you'll be at three o'clock." Then he thought of what he had still to tell them. "No, look, I've got something else to tell you when I've been to thank Alb 'Erratt. How about saying we'll all meet at the Stones?"

"O.K., if you must," agreed Stephen. "But for Pete's sake be careful this time. We'll wait for you at the Stones, and we'll have our grub then. Here, Mark, give him a spear. Now, Rog, keep your eyes on where you're treading—no more sprained ankles—and keep an eye on your watch. We'll all be hungry by three o'clock."

Roger grinned. "Easy. Two eyes on where I tread, another eye on my watch. Easy—only three eyes needed." He added seriously, "I really have got something else to tell you, so be at the Stones at three." He started off down the track by the little brook. "Cheerio. See you later. Look after him, Mark!" he called and then disappeared into the tangle of bushes and tree trunks. Soon the sound of his movements died away. Stephen looked at Mark enquiringly.

"What about cutting across the fields to the Forefinger and following the brook down inside those woods?" he suggested.

"Sure." Mark agreed. "It's a nice little brook, that is. Runs a bit faster than this one. Hope Roger gets back on time to the Stones. We shall be 'ungry by then, an' 'e's got the pudden course." Then he grinned. "No

chance of 'im eatin' it first—I've got the can opener in my
bag." He stood up from the grassy bank he had been
squatting on, dipping his fingers in the trickling water.
"Come on, through here to the field."

The two of them pushed their way through the lush
growth of plants at their feet and plunged in between the
dark, close boles of the oak and birch saplings. Ten yards
in Mark suddenly doubled back and ran again to the
clearing by the spring. He came back to where Stephen
waited. He had his bundle of hazel wands. He grinned.
"Mustn't forget these. We're gunna 'ave great fun wi'
these, you'll see. Come on, follow me."

Roger hated hurrying, and now, of course, he really
knew from past experience how dangerous it could be.
But now he felt that he had better put on his best speed
and get to Alb 'Erratt's cabin as soon as he possibly could.
He did not know whether Alb would be there. He might
be working or have gone away again. Anyhow, he could
always leave the hanky with a note saying thank you,
though it would be better to hand it over to Alb himself.

And so Roger's thoughts sped on as his legs hurried
down the sloping woodland, keeping as near the stream
as possible so as to make sure he did not lose his way.
But he half hated having to hurry. It was all so gorgeous,
so absolutely fresh and natural and unspoiled, exactly like
Narnia must have been, he thought again, as he stepped
from tussock to tussock across a swampy bit of brown
turf where the brook he was following was joined by
another one. He remembered this part from yesterday,

and fairly easily found the way through the squashy soft soil, thankful for his wellingtons. Then a short paddle across the stony bed of the brook and up onto the other bank.

There was that big round pit they had seen yesterday away to his left, as though an exactly circular scoop of earth had been dug out there. He couldn't see why it should be there. He noticed too that the trees thinned out and only young, small birches grew near the round hole. The hole itself had grass and buttercups growing all over and in it. Its floor was about three or four feet lower than the other ground. Roger could not resist jumping down into the hole.

He lay flat out, looking up over the edge. He pretended he had a gun and was shooting at enemies coming up the brook. Perhaps that was it—it was an old gun pit dug during the war, to guard . . . what? No sense in that. There was nothing to guard here. And during the war they had built brick and concrete pillboxes, as they called them, to be gun positions in case the Germans invaded. Roger sighted one final shot along his spear stick, swung his haversack back across his side, and clambered up the side of the grassy hole. Puzzling, but a good place. Nice and sheltered. He would have to ask Mark about it. He trotted on again down the side of the brook.

A quarter of a mile farther on he came to the place where the Middle Finger brook joined the main river, the one that flowed down the Thumb, according to Mark. The water was now wider and deeper. Its noise was a splash and a hurrying, not the tinkling chatter of the smaller brooks. Past here they had not gone the day before, but not very far off, perhaps a few hundred yards ahead, was that sloping tree in the marvelous glade that he had first thought of as Narnia. Roger trotted on, holding his spear in his left hand, keeping his haversack still against his side with his right hand and watching his step very carefully indeed. Nothing was going to go wrong this trip.

The river had cut more deeply into its bed here. He had to leave the bank and find a path some yards away. The thickets were dense, with beautiful straight hazel rods shooting up in thick clumps. He would have to tell Mark about them. They were better here than those Mark had cut—though Roger could not see what he wanted them for. There would be some luscious nuts on these bushes later on. He would love to come back in the autumn.

Then he came to the bed of another stream. It was nearly dried up. Just a tiny trickle of water was moving through the stones, but clearly it had once been a much deeper and wider brook. Roger stepped across and looked up the dried-up bed. As far as he could see it was the same. That would be the stream from the Third Finger, he guessed. Another puzzle, but he could not stop now. He thought suddenly of how short their stay here was— only tomorrow and Friday and then the others were coming to fetch him and Stephen back. There were so many things to find out—but only two more days.

Almost before he had gone on another minute he came to yet another stream. This was wide and shallow and everywhere was very swampy. His wellingtons got very muddy and one nearly came off, so sticky was the wet ground. But at last he was clear of the bog and—his heart gave a leap—there was a long sloping tree just ahead, lying stuck in the fork of another tree, with its roots half in and half out of the ground. It was the rocket birch.

With his pulse thumping madly and his breath coming in gasps as though he were just finishing a ten-mile cross-country race, Roger ran through the greeny-gray trees and came to the holly bush that covered most of the hole torn out when the tree had been half uprooted. With trembling hands he pushed aside the holly leaves. There was no panic this time, just a dull thrill of delight at finding everything just the same. Much greener, more wild flowers everywhere around, and a warmer smell in the air, but essentially exactly the same. There was the black, deep hole where he had hidden, cowering from the man and his dog.

Roger fumbled in his haversack and pulled out his little flashlight. He knelt on the edge of the hole, making the crumbly soil slip down and fall into the darkness. He switched on his light. The pale light was not much good, or else his eyes were too accustomed to the bright light of day. He could see nothing down inside the hole except, after a minute or so, a pale light color on some places where his flashlight shone.

He hesitated. He badly wanted to get into the hole and search around properly inside. Perhaps there were more coins, jewels. . . . On the other hand he had to go a lot farther yet, right down to the Wrist, to Alb 'Erratt's cabin, and then he had to meet the others at the Stones at

three o'clock. He looked at his wristwatch. Phew! Nearly
half past twelve already. He had better get on. He
could leave the exploring of the cave under the tree until
he'd told the others about it. But he might as well leave
his haversack here. It was beginning to feel a bit heavy.
There was no need to cart it all the way to Alb 'Erratt's
and back.

Roger pulled out the red handkerchief, folded it very
carefully once more to make it smaller, and put it into his
anorak pocket. Then carefully he pushed his haversack
tight underneath the holly bush, leaving the strap just
within reach of his fingers so that it would be easy to pull
out. Taking just one more look at the sloping tree and
its hidden root cave, he set off through the thick under-
growth in the direction of the path which he knew led to
the Stones.

When he reached the stepping-stones and remembered
the last time he had crossed them, he could not help turning and looking again at the lovely scene he had thought
so much like Narnia seven weeks before. This time the
magic was still there. The trees and bushes were in full
leaf—he could not see so far between the dense silver
birch boles, and the light was different—but, yes, it was
still Narnia. It was as unspoiled and perfect as anywhere
he knew. He hoped nothing would ever spoil it, ever.

But he must stop dreaming and get on. Mark had said
something about a narrow path by the side of the stream,
going straight on toward the Wrist. Roger turned, left
the Stones behind him, and stepped out for Alb 'Erratt's,
with the chuckling brook at his right hand.

He had not gone far and was just getting used to the zigs and zags of the path when he became aware of a roaring noise of water somewhere ahead. A few dozen more steps and he came to an opening in the woods and saw why the river was flowing so noisily. Its bed was nearly blocked. For some reason great rocks had slipped down from the opposite bank and had piled up in the river's path. The water was splashing and roaring its way past the barrier. It looked as if the fallen boulders had once even blocked the river completely, but now there was a narrow way broken through, about a yard wide, and the stream raced through the gap and fell noisily on to the scattered stones below. It was an exciting, noisy, dangerous place. From high up the far bank a stream ran down to join the main torrent.

Roger was puzzled. Why should there be something like a dam here? Why had the trees faded away all around here? There were only young, small saplings for twenty or thirty yards in every direction before the big trees of the proper woodland size began growing again.

"Better have a look at the top there," he said to himself, and skipped quite safely across the angle of stones until he was on the other bank. The splashing of the water all around him was exhilarating. Another grand place he had found in Left Hand Wood. "I suppose Mark knows all about it though," he said to himself.

He squatted on a handy rock, took out his pencil and map, and briefly marked in the rocky dam on the river's course. He had nearly put the map away when a thought came to him. He opened the folded paper and carefully

121

marked in the other place he had come across earlier on the other side of the rocket birch, the big round hole where he had played soldiers by himself. That done, he began scrambling up the steep, rough slope to see what had happened to cause this landslide into the brook.

The jutting stones made footholds easy to find and he soon found himself panting, on the top of the little gorge. With his back to the river he looked in wonder at the deep round hole just in front of him. A stream trickled into it on the far side, across the stony floor of it and then slipped down to the river the way he had come up. Another round hole—the same size as the other one, only this one was stony and nearly bare apart from odd tufts of grass and buttercups growing in between the stones and a thistle here and there higher up the side of the hole.

Out came the map and pencil again and another find was marked. Then Roger took a last look across the hole, across the waving white heads of the cow parsley beyond the hole. Once again he wished he had a month in which to explore all this fine place instead of just two and a half days, before he climbed and slipped his way down to the river again. Puzzle Hole Number Two—but he must go on.

His watch told him it was nearly a quarter past one. How time flew when you were busy and happy and wanted things to last forever. He began to walk a little more quickly, keeping on this side of the water. Soon the rocky patch ended, the trees around climbed higher and higher, and once again he was in the green half-light and zigging and zagging along the bank. Just past the

end of the fallen rocks, he had noticed another stream joining the main one and he knew from his sketch map that it flowed out of Little Finger. He had not thought about it, but he realized now that it was a good thing to stay this side of the water, as long as the stream did not get too wide or deep to cross when at last he reached the Wrist and had to turn aside to Alb 'Erratt's cabin.

When he reached the belt of pine trees which he guessed must be the Wrist, he had little trouble in crossing the stream. He found a stony patch which he forded quite easily, with the water only halfway up his wellingtons. He could feel the chill of water through the rubber boots. He suddenly felt thirsty. He cupped his hands together and drank several good gulps.

The water was cold and tasted tingling, marvelous, just as everything else around him sounded and looked and smelled marvelous. He wondered momentarily if the water was safe to drink. He could vaguely remember some boys at school who had gone camping in Wales and had been told always to boil water from streams because sheep got into the streams and there was danger of liver fluke. It sounded nasty, whatever liver fluke was, but surely no sheep were allowed anywhere near this stream. He was not sure, but he grinned as he thought with his usual cheerfulness that he had swallowed the water now and what was done couldn't be undone, so why worry? In sheer bravado he stooped and gulped down another double handful.

As he straightened up a sudden idea struck him. He took up another lot of cold water and let it trickle through his fingers. He remembered that Stephen had said all these streams eventually flowed into the River Thames. "Off you go," he said to it. "Go on—down into the big river, and give my love to Big Ben as you go past."

He laughed aloud in sheer pleasure and splashed across to the far bank. He remembered only just in time that he had Alb 'Erratt's red handkerchief in his anorak pocket and managed not to wipe his wet hands on it but dried them on a handkerchief from his trouser pocket instead.

The light and the smell and the feel of the ground were all different when he began walking along the narrow but clear path through the pine trees of the Wrist. Once more this tiny strip of trees had a spring trickling down its length. The path and spring were straight and led direct to a tiny clearing in the trees, where stood a small stone cabin right by the side of the spring, which poured richly from an outcrop of stone near the cabin's wall.

The path led up to the black-painted door. A yard or two away stood a sawhorse with an old band saw leaning against it. Sawdust lay in little heaps on the thin grass and the daisies which scattered the little clearing. The cabin looked solid. The tiled roof was patched, but whole, the single window Roger could see had a bright bit of curtain showing, and from the stubby chimney at the end of the building a thin wisp of woodsmoke wavered upward. It looked as if Alb 'Erratt was at home. Roger walked up and knocked on the door.

12
The Secret Shared

"Come in," called a cheery voice. Roger whirled around in astonishment. The voice had come from behind him. He gasped, "Phew! You made me jump, Mr. 'Erratt. I didn't hear you behind me."

Alb 'Erratt grinned. He was exactly as Roger remembered from the last time: small, neat, gentle, quick and alert and boyish. His white hair was no less startling and was longer than before, and his face in contrast now looked even more sunburned. He put down the old cardboard box he was carrying.

"Been to the village for my groceries." He smiled. "So you're here again, young 'un? I was just behind you the last quarter of a mile."

"You were jolly quiet. I didn't know," said Roger, who felt completely at ease with the man. How could anyone say Alb 'Erratt was strange? Not with Roger, he wasn't. He said, "I've brought your handkerchief back, Mr. 'Erratt, and I wanted to thank you again for helping me that day—properly, I mean. It was all such a rush when the others came, and I never did say thanks properly. . . ."

"Oh, you don't want to worry 'bout that," scoffed Alb 'Erratt. "And don't call me Mr. 'Erratt. Only my dad was ever called that. I'm Alb—short for Albert, if ever you've heard such a soft name. Albert! Imagine calling a little baby, twelve inches long and seven pounds heavy, Albert. 'Tisn't a name for anyone. Still, I got it. But Alb's a bit better, and I'm used to it by now. Thanks for the handkerchief. Nice of you to bother to bring it back. Is your ankle better now? And how'd you know I'd be in this afternoon?"

"I didn't know. Just came and hoped," said Roger. "And, yes, my ankle's fine, thanks. It soon got better. It was only a sprain."

"You come on another picnic with your family, then? Here, come on in. I'll pack me groceries away."

He picked up the cardboard box, tucked it under his arm, pulled a big key out of his old jacket pocket, where it seemed to have slipped into the lining, opened the door and went in. Roger followed him into the cabin. It was lighter inside than he had expected, mainly because of a big window on the wall opposite the door. The view from this window was of tall brown pine trunks close to the cabin with sunlit fields showing in between them. Alb was busy packing the jars and packets into a cupboard that stood just inside the door. A small table by the little window, an old-fashioned washstand with jug and bowl on it, and a plain iron bed with blankets tidily made up completed the furnishings of the cabin, apart from a length of cord matting on the floor and a fireplace of plain stone, where a wood fire was burning dully. Alb shut the cupboard and carefully placed a few small logs on the glowing wood. Cheerful flames crackled up at once. "That's better. I like a bit of fire. Old stone walls like this keep a place cool, you know."

"Yes, I guess so," said Roger, looking around the tiny tidy cabin, fascinated. What a marvelous place to live in—all in the midst of these glorious woods, with a stream right by the very walls. "Lovely cabin you've got, Mr. 'Err . . . Alb, I mean." He corrected himself awkwardly. "We're only staying here for a few days at Burrows' Farm. Mark invited me and my brother. I love it in these woods. I'd love to live in them all the year. You are lucky."

"I don't know 'bout that," Alb chuckled. "You ask the Burrows and the Grays—they think I'm off me head. They don't think I'm lucky. But still, I suppose I am. I like it here, specially now spring's here and summer to come. 'Tisn't so hot in the winter, if you see what I mean. But I've got everything I need here. I'm happy. Keep meself to meself. I'm happy. Got everything I want— have a biscuit—except one thing. They're ginger nuts, my favorites. Get some every Wednesday and there's none left by Friday usually."

He picked up an old saucepan. "I feel like a cup o' tea.

How 'bout you? You got time for a cup o' tea and another ginger biscuit?" He stepped outside to get some water.

"Thanks, yes." Roger was not particularly keen on tea, but he thought it only polite to say yes.

The mention of time made him look at his watch. About two o'clock. He mustn't stay much longer. How long would the tea take to make? Alb 'Erratt came back into the cabin and from his saucepan filled a tiny blackened kettle, which he placed on the now brightly burning fire. "Fresh from my private water tap." He grinned and Roger guessed he meant the tiny spring outside. "Makes a lovely cup o' tea."

Alb sat on the edge of the bed and motioned to the single chair by the table. "Don't stand up." Roger sat down gratefully. "So you're staying with young Burrows. He don't think much o' me, does he?"

Roger was glad to see Alb was still grinning as he spoke. He answered seriously. "He used not to, but I told him how you helped me with my ankle and he . . . well, he. . . ."

"He says I'm maybe not quite so queer as he thought?" Alb put in.

"No," protested Roger. "He doesn't say that."

"O.K., young 'un," said Alb, watching the kettle. "I'm only kidding. I don't mind half so much now what people think about me. Tell the truth, I used to think I was proper queer myself once upon a time, but lately I've been to the doctor's and I feel better than I have for years. That day I met you with your bad ankle, I was just coming back from Cheltenham then. Been to see a specialist"—he tapped his head—"about this. I got knocked about a bit in the war. Got blown up when a bomb went off."

"I know. Mr. Gray told me," said Roger.

"They dug about half a hundredweight of old iron out o' my head, so the Army doctor told me. But they must 'ave missed one little bit—and that'd been causing all the trouble. But they've seen to it now, and I feel fine. Specialist says I'm O.K. Do a good job o' work now. Only one thing I'm miserable about now." He grinned, and lifted up the kettle lid. "Won't be long. Starting to sing, she is." He got up and put out cups and saucers.

"What's that?" asked Roger. "I mean, that you're miserable about?"

"The television." Alb grinned. "While I was in Cheltenham hospital, getting better, they had a telly in the ward. On most o' the time. First I'd ever seen. I thought it was marvelous. Don't half miss it now. Still, it's no good fretting about it. I got no electricity here, so I couldn't plug it in if I could afford a set, which I certainly can't."

"Yes, I see what you mean. I guess I'd miss the good old goggle-box too," Roger said sympathetically. "Thanks." He took the cup of tea and another ginger biscuit. "I'm meeting my brother and Mark at three o'clock. I bet they're not having cups of tea and biscuits."

"Three?" Alb 'Erratt seemed doubtful. "You'll not be going far then?"

"No, we're meeting at the Stones—that crossing place where the others all met me last time."

"Oh, ah."

"Alb . . ." Roger hesitated. "Do you know these woods very well? I can't make out what the two big holes I found this afternoon were."

"Holes? Where?" said Alb, sipping his tea.

"There's one a good bit to the other side of the Stones, and there's one on top of the bank by the sort of landslide, this side of the Stones."

"Ah, I know where you mean—that one, at least. I don't go any farther than the stepping-stones. Another hole up there, is there?"

"Yes," said Roger. "That one's all green and grassy, not like the one at the top of the little landslide. I'd better ask Mark. I expect he'll know." He put down his cup and saucer and stood up. "It's twenty past two—I'd better be going. Thanks for the tea and biscuits, and thanks again for that other time."

"I tell you, you don't want to keep on about a little bit of help like that," Alb insisted. "But it was good of you to bring my hanky back." He walked outside the cabin with Roger, who picked up his hazel spear from where he had leant it against the doorpost. "Have a good time. I reckon you'll be all right for weather. Settled for the week, I reckon—I hope. See you again some time, if you come this way again." The little man seemed genuinely delighted to have had a visitor.

"Cheerio, Alb," said Roger. "I'm off to have my grub now—if the others haven't scoffed it all."

He walked down the little path away from the cabin, turning once to wave his hand and call good-bye to the little figure standing in the lonely doorway.

Once out of sight of the cabin he began trotting. Then, walking fifty paces and trotting fifty alternately all the way where the track was safe enough, he made his way upstream, crossing once more the rushing water at the rock fall, coming to the Stones and finding no one there yet. He hurried to the hidden haversack under the holly bush and then returned to the crossing to wait for the others. He was tingling and nervous with the thrill of what he was going to tell them, and about what they all might find under the roots where he had picked up the Nero gold coin and the mysterious cube of pale blue stone.

How long he sat there daydreaming, soaking in the pleasure of the scene and the sound of water, he had no idea. He had forgotten to look at the time when he began waiting. Then suddenly, *whizzzz*—something flashed across the stream and stuck into the soft earth six feet away from him. *Whizz.* Another, this time closer. He gasped. The missiles were arrows. Each one was white, whittled wood down all its length except for a widening notch end and an unshaped, thicker head.

"That's woken him. Come on, Mark. He's not half a day late this time, anyhow."

With great relief Roger saw his brother and Mark running across the Stones. Each of them carried a big bow, made of some smooth gray wood, and strung taut and bent like a band saw. Each brave had five or six hazel arrows sticking from his duffle bag. They were all carved thin, and shaped like the ones they had shot over the brook near Roger.

"Hiya, Rog." They both seemed in great spirits. They flopped onto the ground by his side, dumping their loads and weapons too. "Like our bows?"

"Super!" breathed Roger. "Where'd you get them?"

"Made them," said Mark.

"That's what those hazel sticks were for then?"

"Yes—arrows, at least. The bows are ash. We went across to the Thumb to cut them. Got one for you." Mark passed a six foot ash-pole to Roger.

"Thanks! Where'd you get your string?"

"Had it with me. You can 'ave some after we've eaten."

Mark was on his knees, fumbling in his duffle bag, laying out the supplies and the vital can opener. The others unpacked their cans and packets and in no time all three mouths were working overtime.

The first course was corned beef wedges between thickly buttered bread, with cheese sections to nibble at the same time if anyone wanted, and spoonfuls of cold beans to help the sandwiches down. When everything except a very few slices of the cut loaf had been finished, the fruit course started—pineapple chunks and cream, with biscuits to taste. The whole was washed down with cups of clear spring water (not from the main river, but from a spring Mark knew nearby), into which Mark dropped some fizzing tablets. Roger and Stephen voted it the best drink they had ever tasted. Mark glowed with pleasure and offered the tablets from the packets he had brought. Soon all three were sucking the tingling little squares and swallowing furiously as the stuff frothed and bubbled inside their mouths.

"Phew!" said Stephen. "What a treat! What a super meal! Had enough, you two?"

"Yes, brother," gasped Roger. "Dinner was late, but dinner was worth waiting for. Nothing left but empties and your bubbly tablets, Mark. Let's pack up. Then I've got something to show you."

The cans and papers were all tidily stowed away and Mark began cutting notches in the ash-pole that was to be Roger's bow. Roger took out his matchbox, slid open the lid and said, "Look, Stephen. Look, Mark. What do you think of this?"

The two boys took one look and stopped whatever else they were doing. Mark let the ash-stick and string fall from his hands as he gasped, "Cor!" Stephen put down his sketch pad and pencil and looked wonderingly at the glinting coin. "Brother! Where'd you find that?" He took the big matchbox from Roger and carefully lifted the heavy coin out of its cotton bed. "Beautiful. Looks brand new . . . but Nero! About two thousand years old and it looks freshly minted. How'd you get it, Rog?"

"That's what I want to tell you about," said Roger, a little breathlessly. "I found it that day we came at Easter and I got my ankle sprained."

"Where?"

"Well, I heard a man and a dog coming, and I thought it was the dog that had been after the sheep, so I hid in a sort of hole by some tree roots, and I found this coin down in the hole. There's a sort of level floor down there. I broke a tiny bit of the stone off—look there—in the corner of the matchbox."

"And you mean to say you kept all this to yourself till now? Seven weeks ago, and it's still a secret . . . didn't tell Dad, or anyone at school?" Stephen was flabbergasted. "It's a marvelous coin, but I don't know what this is." He picked up the tiny cube and fingered it. "Can't make anything out of this, can you, Mark? One side pale blue, the others all like concrete." He looked eagerly at Roger. "Where's the hole, then? Can you remember?"

"Course I can," said Roger. "It's just over there, through those trees, the other side of the path. Come on, I'll show you."

They all got to their feet. Taking care to leave no trace of their meal and picking up all weapons and bags, they filed across the woodland, following Roger, who led them straight to the sloping, half-fallen birch tree.

"This is it. I call it the Rocket Birch, because it's pointed like a rocket, see?" he said. "The hole is around here where the roots have torn up." He took out the flashlight he had been so careful to bring and led the way to the holly bush. He pushed the prickly leaves aside with one booted and jeaned leg and pointed. "There, down there, that's where I hid. I wasn't half scared when the man and the dog came chasing over the brook. I got right down in the hole. The dog nearly found me, but then the man threw something at it and called it off. I'd got my shoe off, so I could feel the coin cold against my foot." He bent down and shone his flashlight into the yawning black pit gaping at his feet. "Are you coming down to search? Might be more coins, and if we find them and they're treasure trove, we get the money they're worth."

135

"Hey, careful," gasped Stephen, as he saw Roger bending forward and peering into the hole. "Don't you go and fall in and break your neck. Come on, I know you. Let's do it carefully. How'd you get in before?"

"Sort of backward," explained Roger. "I'll show you." He turned around and backed toward the hole. He slid his right foot down and then lowered his body until he had gone from sight except for head, shoulders, and a few inches of chest. "That's the first ledge. Then there's another," he said, and to prove his words he moved down until he was quite invisible in the inky dark of the hole.

"You O.K.?" called Stephen anxiously.

"Sure, there's another step, I told you, down onto this level bit, then . . ." The muffled words faded out.

Mark and Stephen peered doubtfully down into the blackness where now they could see the faint yellow flicker of Roger's light as he flashed it around.

He spoke again, and his voice was shaking with excitement. "Come on down and look! Gosh, Steve, it's marvelous. You've never seen anything like it. Gosh!"

Mark and Stephen looked at each other in amazement. Whatever had Roger stumbled on this time?

13
The Dragon's Cave

"Right, we're coming. But shine your light so we can see the steps. Don't want to fall in," called Stephen. "I'll go first, Mark. Then you follow. O.K.?" Mark nodded. "Better pull all our bags and bows in behind that holly bush, so no one can see them. That's better, Rog," he said as he turned and saw his brother pointing the flashlight to indicate the footholds.

Next minute, all three boys were standing side by side gaping in wonder at what Roger's light beam revealed. It was pointing down to the floor, the level smooth floor on which they were standing. The yellow circle of light shone on a gleaming half-moon-shaped picture, a picture made of thousands of tiny red, buff, blue, and white squares, all beautifully designed to show a wonderful leaping, flying dragon. As Roger in wonder moved the light, the twisting body of the beast, with two long, streaming wings curving out, and ending in a many-pronged tail, came into view. All three boys were speechless with amazement.

"Is that a dragon?" said Roger, shakily, at last.

"There're no such things, but if there were, that's what they'd look like, I'm sure," replied Stephen. "Isn't it marvelous? Look at those front claws, those ears flattened back and the wings—you can almost see it moving. And that writhing tail . . . marvelous. And all done in little squares of stone." He knelt down and fingered the picture. "It's wet!" he said in surprise. "And, Rog, that's where your tiny cube of stone came from—look."

Roger moved the light, and saw where about a foot from the intertwining pattern of the border around the dragon, the tiny squared stones had crumbled away and there was a patch of damp earth.

"Any more coins?" asked Mark. "Shine your flash around, Roger."

Tearing their eyes off the dragon at their feet, all three looked at where the flashlight moved. They saw that the patterned floor reached away far in front of them and to the sides. They caught glimpses of many wierd shapes that puzzled and excited them. But what brought gasps from them all was the size of this underground treasure room. Only to the side where the steps led up to the woodland floor and the holly bush was any side wall visible. There it gleamed dully brown. All around the other sides there was apparently no limit to the vault they were in.

"Look up above," Roger suddenly gasped. He had swung his light upward to see how much headroom there was and was astonished at what he saw.

There were hundreds, thousands, countless roots, some brown, some paler, some whiter, all of them twisting and twining and splitting into other tiny rootlets that spread along and in and out of each other in endless interwoven patterns. It was a roof of tree roots, all faintly glistening with dampness. What soil there was above their heads was being kept safely and neatly up above the dense network of roots.

"Cor!" said Mark. "We're under the tree. We're under the roots, looking up!"

"You're right, Mark," said Stephen. "When the tree toppled over, it yanked its roots up and left this space empty underneath somehow. And the tree didn't fall right over, so it's still alive and the roots are growing."

"But what about these pictures?" said Roger. "How did they get here? The coin is an old Roman one. I suppose this is a bit of an old Roman building. Look, there's a bird here." He bent down and traced his fingers around the picture of a brown and white bird about to peck at a plant in front of it.

"Looks like a pigeon," said Mark. "They're a nuisance, eating everything they're not supposed to. 'Ad some o' my dad's peas up already, and—"

"Yes—now look, you two, we'd better be careful.

Keep still a minute," said Stephen. "This is pretty important. We've stumbled onto something big here. I reckon this is the floor of a Roman villa. You remember last year at the Isle of Wight, Roger? Dad took me and Tim with him to see the Roman villa at Brading. You didn't come, did you? Wanted to stay on the beach or something. Well, I reckon this is something like that villa's floor."

"Mosaic," said Roger.

"Yes," said Stephen, "and I reckon it's a marvelous find. But we'd better be careful. This is a cave, and there's no telling how safe the floor is—or how safe that roof is."

"Looks all right," said Roger, and stuck a foot out to try the floor a little farther on.

"I reckon he's right, Roger," said Mark. "I just can't get used to the feeling that there's a dirty big tree growing just up above our heads. I reckoned you 'ad to be dead afore you could look up at a tree's roots."

"We can't leave it without seeing what other pictures there are," complained Roger. "This floor's safe enough. Bit wet though, so let's be careful not to slip. Don't suppose either of you thought of bringing a flashlight?" They hadn't. "Mine's a bit dim. I shall have to get a new battery before we come again. You'd better keep close to me so we can see together."

"O.K., but slowly," insisted Stephen. "Leastways, we can see where the way out is clear enough."

Inch by inch the boys edged forward, Roger and light

in the middle, Stephen to his left and Mark to his right. More pictures and complicated patterns came into sight. One was of a man sitting astride a huge fish. He was holding it by some reins in one hand and he had a trident in the other. An intricate, interwoven border of red and buff leaves curled all around the man and fish. Then, "Look, the Loch Ness Monster!" shouted Roger. And Stephen had to admit it did look like that—a sea beast, snorting water from its nostrils and whipping up the waves with its humped body that curved up and down behind it.

"Phew," said Roger. "Smashing pictures, aren't they?" He moved his light on past the sea monster and found it was shining on a gleaming muddy wall, down which water from the roof above was slowly dripping. Mud had slipped down under the endless drip, drip of moisture and had covered the border patterns just past the sea monster's belly. "Here's the end of the cave," he said, "and that's why the pictures are all so wet. There's water dripping, look."

Slowly they swung around the fading light, and discovered the limits of the cave. Another exciting picture was partly discovered. It seemed to be of a huge scorpion or lobster, but only the front claws and a part of the head were visible. The rest presumably lay hidden farther back behind the earth. To the boys' faint disappointment no more coins were found.

By now the light had become so yellow that they could hardly see, and all three were thinking how pleasant a breath of fresh air would be.

"Your flashlight's had it," said Stephen. "We'd better climb out now. Mark, has your dad got a camera with a flash?"

"No, I don't think so," said Mark, in surprise. "Why?"

"Oh, I'll tell you later. Let's get out. You first, Mark. Then Roger. And go carefully on those little ledges. Don't knock them down. We shall want to get down here again."

"You bet," agreed Mark, and climbed upward.

"No end of exploring to do down there yet," added Roger, following Mark's wellington boots up into the daylight. "No telling what we shall find if we clean away some more of that earth down there. Boy, what a super place this is." He stretched himself up and stepped out from the shadow of the holly bush. He threw his arms upward, then outward toward the still, silver birches. "Left Hand Wood, you're great. Gold coins and Roman ruins, a dragon, and the Loch Ness Monster. Can you beat it? Eh, you two? Can you beat it?"

Somehow the black mouth of the dragon's cave, though mostly hidden by the bushes, gave them all such a feeling of mystery and awe that by consent they moved about forty yards away and then sat down. Stephen was on a tree stump, the others sprawled on the grass, not far from the path down to the Stones, but almost hidden by swathes of bluebell, campion, and yellow nettles from anyone who might pass by.

"Cor, I don't know about you, Rog," Mark said at last. "Don't everything seem to 'appen to you? All that go last Easter—now you go an' find this." And he turned his head toward the Rocket Birch.

Roger grinned. He was thrilled to the very center of his being by what they had found. "Aren't they super pictures though?" he said. "And that whole floor. Why there must be lots more stuff if only we can find it. I mean valuable stuff . . . coins."

"Yes, but what are we going to do about it all?" said Stephen. Roger looked at him in surprise. Stephen sounded anything but excited, almost worried.

"Do? Oh, I see. You mean about getting more batteries for the flashlight—even flashlights for you and Mark —and taking some flash photos."

"No, not that," Stephen said sharply. "It's a good thing you've got me to think a bit for you, Rog. You don't seem to realize what you've been and gone and done."

"Me? What do you mean?" Roger was genuinely puzzled. "All I've done is to find a blessed great hidden Roman ruin and perhaps some treasure. What's wrong with that?"

"Oh, nothing, I suppose," said Stephen. "But you didn't see that Roman villa place at the Isle of Wight. I did. It gave me the creeps."

"What? You weren't scared of those pictures!"

"No, you idiot. Listen. This is Left Hand Wood. It's a lovely place . . . you like it a lot—right?" Stephen leaned forward earnestly.

"Course I do, but—"

"That Roman villa at the Isle of Wight—the floor mosaics weren't half as good as these down there. But there was a big wooden hut built all over them to make sure they didn't get spoiled. There was a little pay-box where you had to dib up a shilling admission and buy a guidebook. There was a big parking lot outside, and they'd made a road through the fields so everyone could drive up and needn't walk an inch—except along the platforms built up round the mosaic floors . . ."

"Oh no!" gasped Roger. "No, they couldn't. Not here!"

"Ah, you see what I mean, then? Yes, how would you like that here, in the middle of this, right here?" Stephen made his point relentlessly. "They'd cut all these trees down here for a parking lot. They'd make Mr. Gray sell them some land so they could build a road down here. They'd build ice cream stands and—"

"We gotta keep it secret," Mark said fiercely.

"Yes," breathed Roger. He looked quite different, his exuberance gone, a boy now beginning to understand how complicated life could be, when it ought to be simple and beautiful. "So we mustn't take any photos, in case the man in the shop that prints 'em tells anyone and—"

"And how can we ask about flashlights back at the farm?" added Stephen. "It's going to complicate life, this is. Brother, you don't half cause things. Still, it can't be helped."

"Steve," said Roger, "I can't quite see who those pictures belong to. I mean, these woods all belong to Mark's dad and Mr. Gray. Well, then, couldn't they just keep them private and not have all those beastly huts and roads and souvenir shops?"

"I dunno," said Stephen. "I don't know much about that sort of thing, except that where there's a really super mosaic they nearly always buy it for the National Trust or something like that. I reckon"—he hesitated—"I reckon we ought to write to Dad and ask him what to do."

"I don't know." Roger by no means sounded in agreement with this. "Once any grown-ups know about it they're likely to spread it about."

"Well, what about your mum and dad, Mark?" asked Stephen. "If it belongs to them, then it might be a bit mean to keep it secret, specially if it's valuable."

"It's no good askin' me," said Mark. "'Ten't as simple as you'd think, is it? An' I wonder how big all the ruins are. I mean, we might 'ave found only a little bit."

"Yes," said Stephen gloomily, "you're right. That other villa in the Isle of Wight was huge. There were lines of rooms, like a blessed great long ranch house. Oh no, we can't have all the archaeologists digging all this up. Look at it. It's too good to be spoiled."

They looked around them. Suddenly the marvel of the beautiful woods seemed threatened, as if a thundercloud had covered the sun.

"Right, then," said Roger. "We agree to keep quiet, do we?" He got up.

"Yes," said Mark, "we gotta."

"Yes," said Stephen. "Yes—at least for the time being. I suppose so."

"O.K.," said Roger. "Now, it's half past four, and it's about time you showed me how you make those super bows and arrows. Then we can shoot them on the way back. I vote Mark takes us back through the fields. Then we'll have better fun, without losing the arrows in the woods."

"Good idea," agreed Stephen.

They collected their haversacks and duffle bags, took the ash bows and hazel arrows, enjoyed one last wondering gaze at the silent, sloping Rocket Birch, and then followed Mark across the Stones, heading for the edge of the Thumb, where he said some good hazel thickets would provide more arrows, before they took to the open fields. After a few hundred yards the dragon's cave already seemed to belong to another world or to a fantastic dream.

At five to six, just as the television news was beginning on the set in the farmhouse living room where Mr. Burrows sat relaxing and waiting for his tea, the three weary boys tramped in. They dumped their luggage on the porch floor and flopped onto any chair they could find in the kitchen, out of Mrs. Burrows' way as she hurried herself, getting the meal.

"Hello, boys," she said, smiling at their tiredness, for she believed that there was no better recipe for health than to go to bed tired out with fresh air activity. "Had a good day?"

"Yep," said Mark shortly, hungrily eyeing the cheese and potato cakes sizzling in the frying pan.

"Oh, marvelous, Mrs. Burrows!" said Stephen. "Absolutely super. I only wish we didn't have to go back to school next Monday. I could explore those woods forever."

"Well, you must come again in the summer holidays,"

said Mrs. Burrows, turning the frying pan's contents over. A delicious aroma of potato and cheese and frying and—when she lifted the lid off the saucepan to inspect its contents—of broad beans spread to every corner of the kitchen and began to make the tired explorers sit up and forget their aching legs and think instead of empty stomachs.

The summer holidays! That jolted Stephen. With a sudden shock it came to him that they had only two more days before they would be collected and whisked back in the car to Cambridge. Then it would be two full months before any more holidays. What about their discovery? How could they possibly leave it two whole months? Someone else might find it. Perhaps they ought to block up the entrance somehow so that it couldn't be stumbled on again. In any case, during the next two days, Thursday and Friday, the big decision had to be made—to keep the secret or to tell.

The thought kept Stephen quiet all through the meal. Food soon loosened Roger's and Mark's tongues and they chattered like starlings about the fun they had had with the bows and arrows, about Roger's visit to Alb 'Erratt, and about what they hoped to do next morning (being careful to keep off the big secret). Stephen only put in odd words, and was so quiet that he twice had to assure Mrs. Burrows that he felt perfectly well and wasn't ill, thank you. He was very glad when the meal was over and he had done his share of the washing up, and all three of them could escape to the garden stile and talk freely.

As soon as he told the others about having to decide

147

one way or the other way about telling Mr. Burrows of the dragon's cave, he could see that Roger was upset.

"We've decided all that," Roger said. "We all promised to keep quiet. It's our secret. No one else need know."

"I'm not so sure we can—not for ever, at least," Stephen said unhappily. "What about all the time we're not here. How's Mark going to guard it all by himself?"

"It's been all right for thousands of years," snapped Roger. "So it'll be all right for a few more weeks."

"You found it—so might anyone else."

"Yes, I found it, so I reckon I ought to decide. And I say keep it to ourselves. You promised. Didn't he, Mark? We all did."

"Yes," agreed Mark. "But—hey—we'd better go over into the field. Dad's just coming out to do some gardening."

They slipped off the stile and walked well out of earshot of the farm. They talked and argued and came to no other conclusion beyond Roger's insistence that he had found the cave and he was the one to say if they should ever tell. Then, slowly, too tired to want to do much more, yet too full of the joy of the lovely evening, they wandered back to the farmhouse.

The last thing Stephen said before they climbed the stile and walked up the slabbed path was, "As early in the morning as we can then. Straight there—and get a flashlight if you can, Mark. Or a box of matches and a candle." Then, because Mr. Burrows, bent over his pea rows, might hear, they said no more. Plans for the following day seemed made. But the moment they stepped into the kitchen Mrs. Burrows called out, "There you are, boys. I quite forgot at tea time. A postcard came for you, Stephen and Roger. Came this afternoon." She held out a color photograph which Stephen at once recognized as the Bristol suspension bridge.

"The Bristolites!" he exclaimed, and turned the card over. His face showed consternation as he read the message part. "Oh, lor!" he groaned, giving the card to Roger. "It's Jane and Sarah. They're coming tomorrow. Mrs. Gray's invited them. Oh gosh, that'll mess everything up!"

14
Ferns, Barrs, and Burrows

"Well! Your poor cousins! What have they done to deserve this?" said Mrs. Burrows in surprise at Stephen's remark.

"Eh? Oh, nothing really, Mrs. Burrows," said Stephen quickly, wondering if he had given anything of the secret away. "No, I meant that we shall have to change our plans a bit, that's all. We've just been out in the field, talking about what we were going to do tomorrow."

"Well, the girls won't get here till the afternoon at the earliest, so you'll have the whole morning to yourselves —provided you get up early and start out at a good time," Mrs. Burrows said. "Are they just coming for the day or longer?"

Stephen looked at the card's message again. "Staying till Saturday, same as us. Then their dad's coming to fetch them on Saturday afternoon."

"Gathering of the clans again," said Mr. Burrows from the porch, where he had been taking off his boots. "Hope you aren't superstitious, Mark. You make thirteen. One thing, I'd say the weather's settled for you all. You must come more often if you bring fine weather like this with you."

After a little more halfhearted chat in the kitchen the boys made their way upstairs to the bedroom Stephen and Roger were sharing. All three sat on the beds and talked about how the visit of Jane and Sarah was going to complicate things.

"Shall we tell them, Rog?" Stephen said.

"I dunno," Roger answered. "If we do, that'll make five who know. It'll hardly be a secret any more."

"If you don't tell 'em," put in Mark, "then there's only tomorrow morning left for everything."

"I know," said Roger desperately. He got up and walked up and down the carpet between the beds. "I suppose we shall have to tell them. Swear them to secrecy. Then there'll be two more to help search the cave properly. He brightened up, having made the decision. "Yes, old Sarah'll keep quiet about it, and Jane too." He chuckled. "I bet they'll be surprised when they see that dragon."

So it was left at that. Stephen still had the uncomfortable feeling that they had only postponed the real decision about whether to tell any grown-ups, but they would have to see what happened in the morning, what new discoveries they made in the cave. For he had no doubt at all they had much more still to find.

Luckily all three boys were tired out by bedtime, dropping quickly off into sound, deep sleep, and so no dreams of flying dragons or snorting sea monsters or snapping scorpions disturbed them.

They made an early start next morning. Not early by Mr. and Mrs. Burrows' standard, but quite early enough by boys-on-holiday standards. Bacon, eggs, and fried bread had been polished off in record time, the haversack and duffle bags filled with all they could think they would need (including Mr. Burrow's car flashlight and three new candles from where Mrs. Burrows kept a store in case of electricity failures), and Stephen had put in his pocket some spare short pencils to be ready for the vast amount of drawing he intended doing. They had not dared to ask about borrowing a camera, because they could think of no reason to give for needing a flash attachment, and an ordinary camera would be useless in the darkness of the cave. Only some snack food for the morning was packed with the other kit, because Mrs. Burrows wanted them home for a proper, cooked midday meal. And, in any case, they all expected the girls would be arriving soon after dinner time, so they would have to go back to meet them.

On their way down the garden path Mark surreptitiously removed his father's hand fork and trowel from the garden shed and stuffed them into his duffle bag. "Can't take anything bigger," he said, looking regretfully at the bigger spades hanging on the racks. "Give the game away, wouldn't it?"

Then it was full steam ahead across the fields and, on Mark's suggestion, not a long arduous tramp through the trees and thickets of the Middle Finger, but instead a quick jog-trot across the spring grassland in between the Middle and Third Fingers.

They were breathless when they had finished the run, and Stephen and Mark both thought they had broken the bottles of pop they were jolting on their backs in their duffle bags, but it was undoubtedly the quickest way to the cave. They had only the two-hundred-yard width of trees to cross when finally they reached the edge of the woods and struck off the path toward the Rocket Birch. The sunlit trees were a glorious sight, standing so gracefully, swaying, with bluebells in drifts about their feet.

Mark had the idea, and it seemed a good one, that they must always scout around before making for the cave, just in case anyone happened to be about. He said hardly anyone ever came that way, except Alb 'Erratt, but it would be better to take no chances. So they went first to the Stones, then along the riverbank each way a few yards and only then to the cave. Once there they slipped behind the holly bush and were hidden in no time.

Down in the dark cavern under the tangled roots Stephen lit all the candles and tried to place them on the floor in three separate positions. He had difficulty in fixing them because the mosaic floor was so wet, and Roger finally had to make a journey "up to earth," as he put it, to find three stones to act as bases for the candles. When this was done and the candle flames had settled to a smooth un-blinking light, the boys began their second exploration of the dragon's cave.

There was no lessening of the marvel. None of them could bear to tear his eyes off the thrilling pictures until he had stared, so it seemed, at every separate one of the countless thousands of tiny stone squares. Now the size of the vault excited them too. The three candles showed up the extent which they had only guessed at the day before, but the candles also with their orange light and the shadows that resulted from the boys' own shapes, made the whole cave seem doubly mysterious.

Stephen soon settled down to sketching the many pictures and patterns and designs. Mark and Roger, one with the trowel and the other with the hand fork, began clearing away some of the mud that was hiding the edges of the mosaic floor. The main difficulty they soon found was that there was hardly anywhere to put the mud when they had cleared it away, for so much of the whole floor was covered with the mosaics. Only a few square feet near the entrance hole had bare earth instead of the smooth, colored stone of the rest of the floor. The mud itself was tricky to handle, and the two diggers had to give up when they found that they were uncovering only inches of new floor while messing up much greater areas with the mud they had moved and with the dirty bottoms of their wellingtons. They had some small luck in finding, in the last handfuls of mud they moved, another coin and a round bead. While Stephen busily sketched, the other two decided to take their finds out into the light to examine them the better.

"Go carefully. Make sure there's no one about," Stephen reminded them, as they hauled themselves up into the sunlight. "Gosh, this dragon's hard to get right."

Just clear of the holly bush they showed each other their finds. Mark's coin was smaller than the one Roger had found and, of course, much dirtier and harder to read. In spite of much rubbing on the grass at his feet Mark could get no clear pictures, heads, or words to read. Roger's find was the heavy bead. A dark-blue, oval stone, it was like a small, smooth, shiny doughnut about an inch and a half across, complete with smooth hole in the middle. Spread equally around the edge were six "eyes," tiny circles of cloudy white with an inside blob of blue.

"Lovely little thing, en't it?" said Mark, his eyes shining with excitement. He fingered his own find proudly. "Soon get this cleaned up when we get 'ome. Hope you're good at reading Roman names. I en't." He grinned and asked, "What we gunna do 'bout digging? Too wet and muddy down there, really, and there's nowhere to put the mud we dig out. Lots more things to find though, I'm sure."

"Yes," admitted Roger, "it's a nuisance, it being so wet. Can't understand it. We've had dry weather all the time we've been here and I know your dad said it'd been dry before that. Why should it be wet under there?" He put the bead into his jeans pocket and zipped it up safely. Then he walked around the other side of the sloping tree, wading carefully through the knee-deep sea of bluebells and yellow nettles. He had gone only a few steps away from the holly bush, with Mark now close behind him, when he stopped in surprise. "It's all wet and swampy here. Come here, Mark. Look, really muddy. Now why? Do you know?"

"Beats me," said Mark. "Ground's not level, the wet ought to drain away O.K. Hey!" he called out. "That's what's making the cave so wet. This swamp is all seeping down there. Funny, I never noticed anything special in the woods up there. Don't go up there very often, though."

"You're right," Roger agreed, bending down and examining the woodland floor. "You can see there, look, just the far side of the tree, it's dry again." He walked across the wet ground until he came to the firm part, and then squelched back. "Now where does all this extra wet come from? Let's track it back and see." He was about to call out and tell Stephen, but decided to keep his voice down, just to be safe. With every passing moment he felt more and more thrilled at the wonder he had found. He was pushing the thought of going home and leaving all the excitement farther back in his mind. "Steve." He knelt at the brink of the cave's doorstep and spoke softly. "Mark and I are just going back a bit up the woods. We think we've found why the cave's so wet. Shan't be long."

"O.K. Not much time to spare, though." Stephen's voice sounded hollow and different from inside the vault. Roger could just see the pale pool of light from the borrowed car flashlight illuminating the snorting head of the Loch Ness Monster. What a pity it was they could not photograph it all. Stephen was good at sketching, but he could not hope to do the marvelous stone pictures justice.

"No, all right," he answered. "Be back soon to do a bit more digging."

He and Mark then began their journey of exploration. Roger walked on one side of the swampy ground and Mark on the other. Between them the wet soil stretched about twenty feet wide in a wandering swathe. Slowly they made their way toward where the band of trees at the bottom of the Third Finger joined the birch glades along the main river's course. Here there were fewer birches with their delicate hanging branches and more oaks, with a few pines scattered among the others.

Roger suddenly remembered where he was. He turned and looked back toward the Rocket Birch. Yes, this was where he had struck that patch of swampy ground when he was on his way to Alb 'Erratt's yesterday. He still couldn't see why this bit should be so wet when the rest on either side was dry.

They went slowly on, and soon Roger began to notice that he and Mark were drawing gradually closer. "You right on the edge, Mark?" he called out.

Mark stepped to his side to check that he was. "Yes. One foot wet, one foot dry, you might say. Are you too?"

"Yes. We seem to be getting a bit nearer each other. Press on."

They pressed on. They had tramped nearly half a mile before they found what they were looking for—the cause of the dampness in the Dragon's Cave. For some time the swampy stretch had been growing narrower and both boys were becoming vaguely aware that what they were doing was following an almost invisible stream back to its source. The fall of the ground here was so slight that the water was seeping far and wide rather than gouging itself a bed out of the soil.

At last, very sticky-booted and quite tired after their wandering trek, they came to the end of their search. The trees thinned out. The sunlight was almost blinding after the shade of the thick woodland cover.

"It's another hole!" gasped Roger. "Well, I'm bejiggered!"

They scrambled up the tiny slope and stood looking in amazement at the perfectly round pool before them. The hole was the same size as the other two Roger had already come across. This one was half full, of clear, cool, slightly rippling water, which was slowly trickling down through a tiny fault in the lip of the hole and disappearing into the swampy path they had followed to find this spot. The far side of the hole supplied the final answer to their puzzle. A tiny stream was trickling into the pool, bringing a constant supply of water from higher up the slope. Somehow—it was beyond Roger's imagination to guess why—this tiny stream had had this mysterious round pool dug out right in its course, so that water first collected in the hole and then slowly seeped out.

"Hey, look," called Mark, who was prospecting around the hole. "This is where the stream used to flow." He showed Roger the tiny stony valley which clearly had once been the bed of the streamlet. It was quite dry, and grass, bluebells, and a few thistles were growing along it. It was several yards from where the water now struggled away.

"Yes, of course," said Roger. "I remember finding this dried-up stream yesterday on my way to Alb 'Erratt's. It joins the main river farther down there, back a good bit

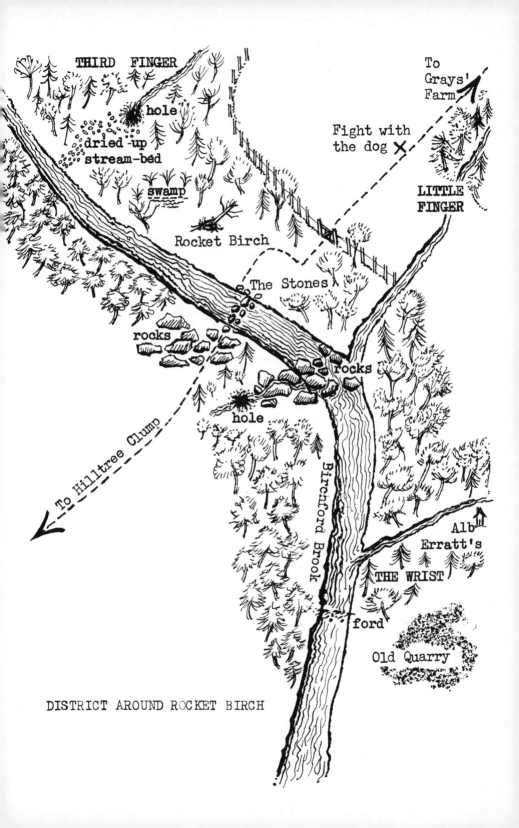

THIRD FINGER

hole

dried-up
stream-bed

swamp

Rocket Birch

The Stones

rocks

hole

To Hilltree Clump

To Grays' Farm

Fight with
the dog ✗

LITTLE
FINGER

rocks

Birchford Brook

Alb
Erratt's

THE WRIST

ford

Old Quarry

DISTRICT AROUND ROCKET BIRCH

from the Stones. But what's happened to do all this? Why'd anyone want to dig a blessed great hole just here?"

There was no answer to that. Both boys searched their pockets for their sketch maps, but only Mark had his. Roger's was back in his haversack.

Then, using sharp sticks to break a new gap in the side of the hole and piling up stones and mud to fill the existing outlet, they did their best to change the flow of the spring back into its original bed. When they had finished, there was a pleasing trickle of water along the little dried-up valley and hardly any dripping into the swampy ground that had for so long been taking the pool's continuous overflow. They tramped back to the Rocket Birch and were so weary and thirsty by the time they got there that their only thought was to get at the bottles of pop and drink the tingling elixir. But first Roger brought his map up to date with the position of the new hole. He penciled *Pool* against it.

Stephen was glad of a break and a drink too. He found the warm sunlight of the birch grove dazzling after the gloom of the Dragon's Cave. He showed them the sketches he had made so far. He had done one rough drawing of the whole floor and separate ones of the Dragon and the Loch Ness Monster. Mark and Roger thought they were very good, but Stephen had the beginnings of a real artist's perception and dissatisfaction. "Can't show the colors, of course," he said sadly. "If only we'd got a flash camera and a color film."

"Maybe the girls will have one," suggested Mark.

"Not them. They wouldn't know how to work complicated things like flashbulbs, not girls." Stephen said scornfully. He added, "I hope they'll help with these drawings though, otherwise it'll take me all day."

"I hope they'll help with the digging," said Roger. "There's sure to be lots more stuff buried under all that mud."

They showed Stephen the bead and the coin they had found already, and he handed them a tiny piece of greenish glass, clearly in the shape of a handle. "I found that just where you'd been scratching away at the wall by the Scorpion's picture. What d'you think it is?"

It was clearly not modern glass, being more opaque than the sort bottles and vases are made of, but that was all they could decide. Stephen rubbed the handle clean and carefully packed it away inside his duffle bag. That reminded them all of the snack food they had brought. All work stopped and biscuits, chocolate bars, and more helpings of pop were transferred from duffle bags to stomachs. They still had about an hour left before it was time to leave and make their way back for dinner.

"Bit of a nuisance, having to go back, isn't it?" said Roger. "There's so much to do and we've got hardly any time left."

Stephen was just going to say that if they had any spare time after dinner while waiting for the girls they could do a useful job bringing all their sketch maps up to date, but he did not get the words out before Roger added, "I'm going to get on with clearing a bit more of that mud away. We tried to alter the way the water was running down to here, but it'll be days before all those miles of swamp dry up." Roger climbed down in the cave, with Mark following. Stephen enjoyed a few more moments of sunlight, sighed at the thought of how inadequate his drawings really were, made up his mind that he would start saving up for a decent camera that could take flash photographs, and then descended into the cave.

The candles, now half burned down, flickered capriciously as the three boys moved about the cave at their tasks. It took many minutes for their eyes to become used to the gloom after the brilliant spring sunshine that dappled the woods up above them. Stephen found the colors of the mosaics harder and harder to make clear. He was using ordinary black pencil, but he was trying by various shadings to show which parts were one color and which were another.

The pile of earth and mud and stones which Roger and Mark had moved was now nearly as big as they could manage to confine to the tiny patch of ground not covered by the mosaics. Roger was wondering how to get rid of some of the spare soil and thinking in terms of borrowing some old washing-up bowls or buckets from Mrs. Burrows (though how was he to explain why he wanted them?) when his trowel struck something hard. He dug into the mud wall again. This was something more than a stone. He worked hard, but carefully, because he had the sense to realize that whatever he had found might be very fragile. He called over Mark, who began scratching away with his hand fork to try to uncover the mysterious find. Soon it was clear that it might be something important, and Stephen moved over to hold the big flashlight so that the miners could see better. But again they were defeated by lack of space. There was nowhere to put the soil and mud they were clearing away from around the big, black, slightly rusty, smooth object they were slowly uncovering.

"Blast," said Roger for the tenth time, as he slipped on the muddy floor. "This is hopeless. Can't get at it properly, and it's making a mess of the floor. We'll just have to get some buckets or something."

"Yes, but what is this thing?" said the puzzled Stephen. He smoothed his fingers along the curving black side. "It's metal, I think, but what's it supposed to be?"

About fifteen inches were clear of the surrounding soil, but the bottom and top were still hidden. The thing sloped at an angle of about forty-five degrees.

"Here, let me have that trowel a minute," said Roger suddenly. He dug away a few more handfuls of soil from the bottom and said in satisfaction, "Yes, I thought so. Look, there's where the base comes."

Stephen held the flashlight closer and, sure enough, the flat, apparently circular rim of the thing's end was partly revealed.

"Queer," said Mark. "But we shall 'ave to go back soon. I'll try and nick a bucket out o' dad's gardening shed this afternoon. Then we'll be able to throw some o' this spare muck out o' the way and get at this thing a bit better."

"If we do, we'd better be careful to look through the soil jolly carefully first, before it's thrown away," said Stephen. "You know proper archaeologists sift everything to make sure they don't miss anything."

"Have a job to sift this mud," grunted Roger, who was still clearing away the clinging soil around the thing. "It's jolly big and solid, whatever it is. Blast! There's just nowhere to put the soil."

Stephen checked his watch. "We'd better go back. Mark's right. If we can get a bucket, that should help with the problem. Come on, Rog, tear yourself away. Gosh, Mark," he added, chuckling, but with a tinge of awe in his voice, "I wonder what he's found this time?"

"Ah, he's the one for findin' things, en't 'e?" Mark said admiringly. "Has 'e always been like this?"

"No, quite normal till he fell into that bramble bush last Easter Monday."

"Ah, must 'ave been something in those thorns, eh?"

They chuckled to each other, Roger did not mind. He straightened his aching back. "You can say what you like, you two, but I reckon this is something bigger than all the rest put together. Yep, something terrific. You see. You just see."

Stephen sighed, "Yes, I'm not betting, but I guess you're right. You can't help it, I suppose, but, brother, how things seem to happen when you're around! I'm not sure you're safe to know. Come on, pack up and let's buzz off to the farm. The girls are coming, remember." They climbed out of the Dragon's Cave into the world above.

It was lucky for Roger's state of mind that the girls were not late in arriving. Now that he had something really exciting to dig up, Roger was finding delays and interruptions for meals and washing up and waiting for cousins almost unbearable. But Mr. Gray drove up into the yard of Burrows' Farm a few minutes before the big after-dinner washing-up session was finished, surprising Mrs. Burrows and delighting her son and his guests, who eagerly threw down drying-up cloths.

"Here they are, Molly," said Mr. Gray, coming cheerily into the kitchen, followed by Jane and Sarah. "Hello, boys. Enjoying your holidays? These two cousins o' yours couldn't get here quick enough. Wouldn't have more than three helpings of pudding, but must rush over here as soon as possible." The boys grinned at the protests the girls began blurting out. Mr. Gray said he couldn't stay, but would fetch Jane and Sarah back after tea. "Or, if you're down our way, just come across the fields. You remember the way from last Easter, don't you?"

Five minutes later the five were trotting down the field toward the tip of Middle Finger. Mercilessly they made Sarah hurry the whole way down the path outside the woods, and finally all arrived, breathless and exhilarated, at the edge of the trees, as near as they could reckon to the Rocket Birch.

"O.K. Rest here a bit," gasped Stephen, and they all threw themselves down on the grass and buttercups.

"Will someone tell me what—what all the rush is for?" puffed Sarah. "And why've we brought a bucket?"

"Yes, what's going on, you lot?" Jane chipped in. "I wanted to go through the woods, not practice for the marathon across these fields."

"Something terrific, Jane. Something great. Roger's

been at it again. But first, before we tell you, you've got to promise to keep the secret."

"Yes, a real sacred promise," insisted Roger. "No mention of it to Mary, Anne, or Peter or your mum and dad."

"Or Auntie and Uncle Gray," added Mark.

"Simply say nobody," said Stephen. "You must promise to tell nobody. Will you swear that?"

"I'll promise anything if it's not any more running," said Sarah.

"No, we're serious, Sarah," insisted Stephen. "Come on, you two. Stand up." The girls obeyed, mystified. "Hands on your hearts. Do you swear on your honor to keep this secret?"

"Yes," said Sarah solemnly, impressed by the boys' tone and seriousness.

"Me too," said Jane. "But what *is* the secret?"

"Lead on, Rog," grinned Stephen. "You found it. You show 'em."

The Indian file threaded its way through the woodland. The girls gasped with delight at the loveliness of the spring scenes that unfolded as they walked on. The boys insisted on hurrying. Very soon the girls were tingling with the excitement they felt transferring itself from Roger, leading the procession, and Mark and Stephen in the rear. At last they came to the glade where the Rocket Birch stood, sloping silently, as sentinel to the treasure hidden at its roots.

"This is it," said Roger casually, his eyes twinkling.

"Where? What?" said Jane puzzedly.

"Can't you see it?"

"No. What?"

"You mean you really can't see it?" chuckled Stephen, enjoying the joke.

"Blind, en't they?" grinned Mark.

"Come off it, you lot," scoffed Jane. She sat down and leaned back. "What's all the mystery? And what's that blooming bucket for? Ow!" She had leaned back too far and found the holly bush pricking her neck. "Ow, that's sharp!"

The boys howled at this. "Can't you see it yet?" choked Stephen. "Mind you don't fall down it."

Jane stood up hurriedly. "Fall down what?" She looked around, but could not understand what the boys were finding so funny.

"All right. I'll show you. Watch what I do and follow on. O.K.?" Roger grinned happily, enjoying himself hugely. He pushed past the holly bush. Sarah followed. What had he done this time? She gasped as she saw the gaping mouth of the cave. "What's that?"

"The Dragon's Cave," Roger said, and slipped down into it.

"Dragon! Where?" Sarah stood hesitant on the brink, peering into the blackness. Jane and the boys were now at her elbow. "Jane, Roger says this is a dragon's cave."

"Come on, jump down," came Roger's voice. "I'm shining the flashlight on the steps. It's easy."

Sarah gingerly turned around and stepped cautiously down. She was relieved to find a smooth floor beneath her feet at last. Jane followed, then Mark and Stephen.

"All down? Now, Jane, Sarah, you want to close your eyes hard for a few minutes so they get used to the dark, and don't look toward the doorway. Turn your backs on it and look down here when you're used to the light— down on the floor." They did as Roger told them. Then he switched on the big car flashlight. "Now, what do you think of this? Isn't it fantastic?"

Once again Roger glowed to hear the astonished gasps caused by the sight of the mosaic beasts on the twinkling floor at their feet. It was great to have a secret like this, but it was very pleasant too to see how people reacted when you shared your discovery with them.

"It's so . . . so real," whispered Sarah, kneeling down and fingering the smooth stone squares in wonder. "It's beautiful . . . marvelous."

"How did you find this, Rog?" said Jane faintly. "Fell down the hole, I suppose."

"No, not exactly. This is where I hid when I thought it was Alb 'Erratt and his dog coming after me."

"I don't know about you, Rog!" Sarah's admiration was boundless. "Everything seems to happen to you."

"That's what everyone says," Roger grinned in the dark.

And so the wonderstruck girls inspected the pictures one by one. The Dragon, the Loch Ness Monster, the Scorpion ("Lobster?" queried Jane), and the Pigeon were all gaped at, gasped at, and whistled at. "And that's Neptune, I suppose," said Jane, admiring the picture of the man with a trident, on the back of the monster fish. "It's a real treasure house. Is the roof safe, do you think?" She looked doubtfully up at the tangle of roots.

"Yes. And we've found some coins and other things too," said Roger, and the girls were shown them in the light. Roger took new candles from his pocket and lit them, leading the girls over to the corner where the big black rusty thing was gradually being uncovered. "And we don't know what this is. That's what we brought the bucket for."

"What?"

"To cart away the spare soil in. There's nowhere to put it down here. All the floor is covered with the mosaics."

He led them around the whole cavern, like a museum curator proudly showing his collection, the candle in his hand flickering so much that Jane did not see the pile of mud and fell over it. She only got her hands and the knees of her jeans messy, but what she hated most about the tumble was that she found herself on her knees, her face and the Dragon's snorting nostrils only a few inches apart. She hurriedly scrambled to her feet.

"Why is it so wet, Rog?" she said.

Roger explained about the stream which had gotten diverted farther up the woods and had been seeping into the cave. Jane was still puzzled.

"But all these pictures look so new. They can't have had water sloshing across them like this for thousands of years, can they? They'd be all worn away."

"It's only been dripping down the wall there, and sort of oozing across the floor," said Stephen. "But I reckon you're right. They'd have worn away in all those years."

"How old is it, do you think?" asked Sarah. "I mean, the Romans left this country hundreds of years ago . . . so . . ."

"I don't know about this building, but Roger's coin's got Nero on it, and he lived about 50 or 60 A.D., didn't he? The Fire of Rome, Saint Peter and Saint Paul in the arena and all that?" said Stephen doubtfully. He liked Roman history and now wished he had learned a bit more. None of the others felt able to say whether he was right or wrong.

"Gosh, that makes it terrifically old," said Sarah. "What are you going to do about it? I mean, all the history professors and the archy-what's-its-names . . ."

"Archaeologists," said Jane knowingly.

". . . yes—will be thrilled to bits about this."

"We haven't decided what to do, really," said Roger. He hurried on over that awkward point. "But we haven't got much time left. Only today and tomorrow, so what about getting on with the digging? Going to help me, Sarah?"

"Sure, I will. And Roger—Stephen—Mark . . ." She hesitated.

"Yes? What?" Roger said, surprised at her shy tone.

"Thank you for telling us about this cave. It's the most exciting thing in my whole life."

"Oh, that's O.K.," said Roger awkwardly. He wanted to stop talking and get on with the scratching and scraping to uncover the thing in the corner. He wished Sarah wouldn't gas on. "You and me and Mark do the digging. And, Jane, Stephen said he wanted you to help him copy the pictures."

In this way the afternoon shift began. All five worked as hard as ever they had in their lives. The digging was painfully slow and tedious, because every bucketful of soil had to be taken up above and tipped out, to keep the excavations around the "Thing" clear. Before half the afternoon had gone, Jane and Stephen were helping in the mining and carrying and the tipping out. It was hard work, and soon all of them except Roger had had enough. They were sweating furiously, their hands and arms and sleeves and knees were filthy with mud. Jane and Mark had at some time wiped their sticky, muddy hands across their faces, with the result that they had streaky, sweaty dribbles of brown running from their foreheads to their chins. Worst of all, the mosaic pictures were getting terribly smeared.

"Come on, Roger," called Stephen at last. "Pack it in. Let's have a rest and a cleanup down at the brook." The others eagerly agreed. The thought of the cool, splashing water down at the Stones was refreshing in itself.

"O.K.," Roger agreed wearily. "Anyhow, the candles are about done for. But I've got half the base just about clear. I reckon there's some letters on the bottom."

"Leave it now. Bring the bucket, and we'll get some water to clean the floor with. Come on."

Roger heard the four of them walking away. He wearily blew out the candle stubs, picked up the flashlight, and climbed out. He felt utterly exhausted and dirty all over, but completely determined to get the mystery Thing clear of the mud and up into the daylight. He felt sure it was something really special, a statue perhaps. The bit they had dug clear would be the base. If only they had better tools. Still, must be careful and not miss any small things like coins and so on that might be lying around. He stiffly followed the others down to the Stones.

15
The Holes

By six o'clock that evening all the miners were beginning
to feel stiffness coming on, caused by the unaccustomed
labor and continual bending down in the Dragon's Cave.
They had decided after their cleanup at the Stones that
they had better go back for tea, and also for some more
candles or flashlight batteries, if Mark could again successfully manage to burgle his mother's emergency candle
store. Now sprawled about the sitting room after a lovely
tea, none of them felt much like starting work in the cave
again, except for the determined Roger, who tried to rouse
them and get them moving again. Finally in desperation
he had to say, "Well, I'm going. If you lazy lot want to

sit about and let your life waste away, I don't. Anyone else coming?"

He was going out of the doorway when Mark jumped up and followed, clearly much to Roger's relief. Together they pocketed candles and matches and left. Stephen grinned and said, "We'll follow on in a few minutes. But I want to get my sketches tidied up and the maps made up to date first."

The drawings of the mosaic pictures were sorted out first. Jane and Sarah thought they were good, but Stephen wasn't very thrilled. He was still thinking in terms of color photographs or slides. Next he showed his cousins the sketch map. He told them how Left Hand Wood had gotten its name, what the various bits and pieces marked on the map were and then said, "I'd better put in these mysterious holes old Rog keeps on about. Mark and I found one in the field where we had our archery practice yesterday." He bent over the map and marked a tiny circle where he reckoned the hole was and then he had a sudden thought. "Sarah, see if Roger left his haversack in the hall on the coatpeg. If he has, see if you can find his map in one of the pockets." Sarah soon returned with a crumpled piece of paper.

"Is this it? That's all the paper he's got in his bag."

"Yes, thanks. It's gotten a bit grubby." Stephen flattened out the map and then pointed.

"There . . . and there . . . yes, look, he's written *Hole* by each one. Let's see . . . One is halfway down the Middle Finger, not far from the brook. I remember vaguely seeing that the first time we went down there. That's the one marked in. Now, the other, there, farther downstream, right on top of the bank. And there's a landslide there, so Rog says. Hey . . ." His voice trailed off in surprise. "There's another one . . . not far from the Dragon's Cave. Oh yes, I think he and Mark did say something this morning about finding out why the cave was so damp. Can you read this scribble, Jane?" Stephen passed the map over. "Look, what's he put by that circle?"

"*Pool*, is it?"

"Might be. Silly, why doesn't he make it clear. First rule of map making. Oh, well, I'll put it in. H'm, that makes four mysterious holes. Wonder what they are?"

The girls bent down and peered at the map.

"Jolly good name, Left Hand Wood, isn't it?" said Jane.

"Looks exactly like a bony hand," agreed Sarah.

"Ah, yes, and I've got Alb 'Erratt's cabin to mark in," said Stephen, and made a neat hole by the tiny stream in the Wrist. "Funny about those holes. Queer, aren't they?"

"Queer? What's queer?" Mr. Burrows' deep voice from above startled them. The three cousins were kneeling on the rug, noses down to the map, bottoms in the air, and they had not noticed him come into the room. They stood up, and Stephen showed Mr. Burrows the sketch map of Left Hand Wood.

"Looks a pretty good map. Well drawn. Nice and clear," commented Mr. Burrows.

"Can you tell us what those holes are, Mr. Burrows?" said Stephen.

"Holes? Where?"

"There are four of them, starting there in the fields."

"Oh, that one in Boundary Field. Oh yes, I can tell you who made that." Mr. Burrows chuckled.

"Who?"

"The Jerries. German bomber, one night in the war. Aiming at the airfield up on the hill, I suppose. Rotten shot, wasn't it?" About a mile wide. That's what that hole is—a bomb crater."

"I see! Thanks, Mr. Burrows, that's a mystery solved. I guess these other holes are bomb craters from the same plane. They're all in a straight line, or more or less."

"Might be," admitted Mr. Burrows. "Long time ago, but I only reckon I ever thought there was just the one bomb. Course, that's the only one I ever saw the hole for. If the others dropped in the woods, I shouldn't 'ave seen anything. Hardly ever go there." He picked up the newspaper he had come in for and went out.

"Bombs!" said Jane in anger. "Fancy bombs going off in those lovely woods! I'm glad it was a long time ago. I'd hate to have seen all the damage to the trees."

"Yes," said Stephen slowly. "That accounts for the empty spaces all around these holes too. Rog said the trees thinned out around the ones he saw, and that's why, I guess. The explosion blew all of them down, and only new saplings have grown up since."

"Twenty years ago," said Sarah. "Just think, these holes have been there twenty years, and no one's found out till now. Did Mark know?"

"No. We asked him. He just said, 'Holes? I dunno. They been there all the time I been about. What d'you

176

mean, how'd they get there?'" Stephen gave a passable imitation of Mark's breathless, rushing way of speaking and the girls smiled.

He was looking at his map of Left Hand Wood. He pointed to the empty space up above the Thumb, Forefinger, and Middle Finger. That's where the airfield is. These bomb craters are certainly a good long way off." He traced the direction of the line of holes, "One or two more bombs in the same line—just supposing the plane was going north—and one would've landed right on this farm."

"Lucky they fell in the woods, really," said Sarah. "Safest place by far."

"Hadn't we better get going after the others now?" said Jane. She was keen to get back among the trees and the lush growth of the woods, to say nothing of tackling the puzzle of the big black Thing in the Dragon's Cave.

"Hang on a minute," said Stephen huskily. The girls stopped and looked curiously at him.

"What's up?" said Jane.

"These holes—bomb craters. Look how they're spaced," said Stephen breathlessly.

"What about them?"

"These three, all the same distance . . ."

"If your map is right," interrupted Jane.

"It is," snapped Stephen. "I copied the distances and positions very carefully from the proper printed map, so they're near enough exact. Now, three all the same distance apart. Then the last two—twice as far apart as the others. See?"

Peering at the map, both girls finally agreed.

"So what?"

"Bombs were dropped in batches. I remember Dad telling me about the plane he used to fly in. It had a gadget to space the bombs out, so that they didn't all fall at once but spread out in a line. A 'stick' of bombs, they called it."

"Yes, but—"

"Well, don't you see? There's one bomb crater missing. There ought to be another hole in between these two."

"Where?"

"Halfway between." Stephen put his pencil point on the sketch map.

Jane said, "Can't be there! That's where the cave is." Stephen looked at the neat printing by his pencil point.

"What? Oh, my gosh! Yes!" Stephen was white faced. He struggled to his feet. The girls were alarmed. They had never seen fright showing in anyone's face like this before.

"What's up?" wailed Sarah. "What's wrong. I don't understand."

"There's no hole around there! We looked all around the cave, so the bomb can't have gone off like the others did. Don't you see? There must be an unexploded bomb somewhere there, in between those last two holes, and it'd be just where the cave is. And Roger's down there hacking away at a dirty big rusty black thing! That's what that statue of his really is, an old German bomb!"

Jane let out a big whistling breath. Sarah wailed again, "Oh no! Poor Roger! What can we do?"

Stephen, still white as paper, said decisively, "Get down to the cave and warn him and Mark as soon as we can. Come on, Jane, we shall have to run. Can't get a car down there. Anyway, if it's all a false alarm, we wouldn't want to have told Mr. Burrows for nothing."

"What about me?" Sarah gasped as she followed the hurrying pair out into the garden.

"Keep up as long as you can with us, but we've absolutely got to fly," yelled Stephen. Jane and he ran on.

Sarah watched them vault the stile into the field and race away toward Middle Finger. She stood, hesitating, knowing she could not keep up with the pace their long legs would set but desperately wanting to do something, anything, that would wipe away the dreadful feeling of disaster that had swept over her. Poor old Roger . . . in a cave with a blessed great bomb. And Mark . . . whatever would Mr. and Mrs. Burrows do if Mark was killed? All these agonizing thoughts flew through her mind, and then she turned, sobbing under her breath, "Sorry, Rog, but I've got to break my promise. I've just got to." She ran frantically back to the farmhouse, dashed into the kitchen, and poured out the whole story to an incredulous Mr. and Mrs. Burrows.

Stephen was praying silently as he pounded down the home field toward the first of Middle Finger's trees. "Please, God, don't let it explode. Please, God, don't

let Roger set it off. Please, God, make the silly idiot
see what it is and leave it alone." His feet pounded over
the soft turf and his eyes looked ahead for obstacles to
avoid. His lungs began to burn and to feel as if they must
burst, and he could feel his heart beating like a mad drum-
mer. All the time he was expecting to hear the dull roar
of an explosion that would make his headlong rush a waste
of time. He could imagine Roger and Mark kneeling
down in the dark cave and eagerly digging, pulling, lever-
ing at the big black thing, all the while believing it to be
a statue, never dreaming what it really was.

The tip of Middle Finger was well behind them now.

Jane had fallen a few yards behind. Wasn't keeping up badly for a girl, thought Stephen. He wondered whether Sarah was following. Over his shoulder he breathlessly called, "Keep it up, Jane. Nearly there."

They raced up to the bend in the footpath where it turned toward Grays' Farm, but they kept straight on, on, on down the tilting, bounding field by the side of the long band of oaks that made Middle Finger. Stephen felt the stitch coming on. He wished he had started off a bit more slowly. He was stupid to try to sprint the whole mile or more. He tightened his stomach muscles, forcing the pain of the stitch back, as he had found he could do on the school cross-country runs. He had never thought he would be glad for those beastly, muddy, cold runs across the fields at school. Now he wished miserably that he had done more. Then his rotten legs wouldn't burn so much, and his mouth and chest wouldn't feel on fire. On and on—left, right, left, right—he forced himself to go faster than his body wanted, until the field, the trees, the sky, all bounced up and down in time with his pounding feet and he felt that nothing would ever be still again.

The trees were coming nearer at the far end of the field. Jane was now fifty yards behind. She had tripped on a molehill once and gone sprawling, but now she was running again, sobbing with anxiety. The trees of Third Finger were coming nearer on the left. Not long now. Stephen thought dully that he was getting so dazed—all he could hear was his heart drumming away and his breath rasping in and out—that he would never hear a bang now. "Please," he thought, "please, God, let old Roger and Mark get tired and leave off digging."

The first trees swept up. There was barbed wire. Throw yourself full length under the bottom strand and wriggle through. Stagger up and force your legs, that wanted so much to wobble and collapse, to start running again. Curse the twists in the track. Curse the bushes. Blast the branches slashing across your face, the hollies clutching at your jersey, the stones twisting your foot. On, on, dodging across clearings, jumping tiny streamlets, squelching in muddy patches. *Muddy patches*—must be near the cave. Yes! Oh, thank God, there's the tree. Force your legs on. Don't fall flat on your fool face with only twenty yards to go. Give them a shout. "Rog!" Only a faint croak. Yell louder, you fool! "Mark! Come out of there!"

Flinging his way past the holly bush, nearly tumbling headlong from exhaustion into the cave, Stephen gasped into the darkness below, where he could see the candles crazily jerking up and down. "Get out of that cave, you two. Quick! *Out* of the *cave!*"

Two startled, pale faces jerked towards him.

"What's up, Steve? About time you got here. We were—"

"Get out of the cave. Get . . ." Stephen's breath was too uncontrollable for more than one brief shout at a time. He gathered all his strength and shrieked in a frantic yell that Jane, only just entering the wood scores of yards behind him, could hear. "*OUT*! That blasted thing's not a statue—it's a *bomb*. Get out, you stupid *idiots*!"

There was an endless moment of utter silence in the cave below him, then a frantic scuffling as first Mark, and then Roger, eyes wide as saucers with incredulous alarm, clambered up the worn steps and rushed after the retreating Stephen and Jane into the safety of the close-set trees near the path to the Stones.

16
No Other Way

"Blimey! A bomb! Are you sure, Steve? . . . Yes, o'course it's obvious now, en't it? . . . An' we thought it were a statue!" Mark sat down heavily on a handy stone. "Oh, lor . . . I been pulling and shoving and banging it all over the place—and all the time . . . Cor!" For once in his life the loquacious Mark was startled into silence. He and Roger had heard Stephen's worried explanation and had been forced to the same conclusion, that the Thing was no long-lost Roman treasure, but a twenty-year-old product of Krupps, left behind by a pretty poor bomb-aimer of the *Luftwaffe*. They were mightily impressed when they found that Stephen and

Jane had run all the way from the farm to warn them, and shakily thanked them.

"All the same, Steve, if it's been there twenty years it's probably safe by now," said Roger. This latest development had shaken the foundations of his whole happiness. For months now he had dreamed of what the cave might hold. All the dreams had been realized, and for the past forty-eight hours he had been thrilled as never before. Now, cruelly, everything seemed likely to be blown up in ruins at any moment.

"No, I reckon the longer bombs lie about the more likely they are to go off . . . That's what I read somewhere." Stephen stared dully down the path. "What are we going to do, Rog? Don't you think we've got to tell someone about that thing down there? Because if it is a bomb then all this part of the woods is unsafe. You know how they close whole streets and move people out of their houses when they find old unexploded bombs in London."

"Where's Sarah?" said Jane. She had said very little since the four of them had stumbled in something near panic from the cave, excepting when she had backed up Stephen's gasping reasoning about the gap in the stick of bombs, the missing hole, and what that meant.

"I dunno," Stephen said. "Thought she was following us. Can't have done though, or she'd have been here by now." He paused. He stood up and beckoned to them all to be quiet. "Can you hear someone coming?" he whispered.

Everyone could. At least two people were coming

along the path from the direction of Grays' fields. Their voices and footsteps were quite clearly heard in the near silence of the woods. The four listeners slipped quietly into hiding in the thickets near the path and waited anxiously.

"Hey, look!" Roger hissed in Stephen's ear as they crouched behind a hazel, "It's Sarah . . . and Mr. Burrows too. Oh, gosh, that's done it!"

The four children rather awkwardly appeared from their hiding places, and Sarah in great relief gasped, "Oh, so you're all right then!" And Mr. Burrows said quietly, "Thank the Lord! I've never been so scared in me life. Is it all true, what this lass's been telling me? We came in the Land Rover down the fields. No kidding now. Really a bomb somewhere in there, is there?"

"I'm afraid so, Mr. Burrows," said Roger. "We're pretty sure it is. The way Stephen puts it, it can't be anything else. All those holes, in an exact line . . ." He stopped breathlessly. Now things were really getting out of control. A grown-up knew. All the glorious secret was out and the shine had gone off the world.

"Has Sarah told you about the cave, Mr. Burrows?" asked Jane. "I mean, about the . . . ?"

"The pictures on the floor? Yes, though I can hardly believe that either. Who'd 'ave thought that these ol' woods had kept two secrets like that all those years. Proper marvel, I reckon."

Mr. Burrows' face was worried. He scratched the bristles on his chin. He had been halfway through his evening shave when Sarah had rushed in with her electrifying news, and now he had one side of his face smooth and the other side and his chin still bristly. His eyes twinkled and he slapped Roger on the back suddenly, making him jump with the surprise and vigor of the thump. "Eh, boy! What a one you are for getting mixed up in things! All that do last Easter, now this! People'll be saying you aren't safe to know!"

He smiled and put an affectionate arm around Mark. "Been trying to get blown up, eh?"

Roger grinned weakly, "I know, Mr. Burrows. I feel awful about this, especially as we don't seem to be sure what to do now."

"I reckon there's only one thing to do," said Mr. Burrows dryly. "Before I ring up the police, or the Army, or the Prime Minister or anybody and tell 'em we've got a bomb in our woods, well, I'd better be sure it *is* a bomb. What's it look like, Mark?"

Mark and Roger told him. Stephen and Jane confirmed the descriptions and said they were quite sure it was nothing like an old oil drum or anything like that, that someone had dumped there as rubbish. Anyway, they said, the Thing had been fully buried five or six feet under the ground when Roger had first found it by hitting his trowel blade against it. Roger looked at Mr. Burrows when he heard that bit and wondered if he could see how scared he felt now at the thought of what might have happened if that trowel had set the bomb off.

"Right," said Mr. Burrows. "Now get this straight. You all stay here except Roger. He can show me the first bit of the way and then I'll have a gentle look and see if I think it's a bomb. After that we'll see. Have to tell Jeff Gray. Anyway, we'll go back up that way. My Land Rover's by the old gate along the end of this path. Now—stay put. Come on, young Roger! Let's get going."

Together they strode off into the birch woods, Roger's slim figure trotting after the broad, solid form of the farmer. Roger had to go nearer than Mr. Burrows intended, for without being shown exactly where to go he would never have found the cave. At the brink he ordered Roger back again, took the flashlight and slipped down to look at the Thing. He was down for ages, it seemed to the anxious four, waiting up on ground level. When he did reappear, he looked thoughtful. There was a strange, excited look in his eyes.

"I reckon it's a bomb, all right," he said in answer to the anxious enquiries when he reached the path. "Now, those pictures. I see what you mean, you five beauties. I really do. We can't have those marvelous things blown up. They're wonderful." He said again, full of disbelief, "To think I've been around these woods forty years, and I never found anything more exciting than a buzzard's nest or a dead beer bottle, and you come here for a day or two and find all this!"

They walked back to the Land Rover, and drove slowly and bumpily up the steep fields to Grays' Farm. Roger whispered to Sarah just before they got out, "It's O.K., Sarah. You had to tell. Thanks for coming after us."

Sarah smiled with relief that Roger was not angry. "I didn't know what to do. All I could think of was you and Mark getting blown up . . . so I simply had to tell Mr. Burrows."

"It's O.K.," he said. "Really it is. At least Mark and I aren't lying about in bits. But I don't know what's going to happen now."

Mr. and Mrs. Gray were astonished at what they were told, although they had been prepared for some surprise by seeing the Burrows' Land Rover hurrying down the fields. They too looked again at Roger with an expression of wonder, and asked many questions about the cave: how had it been found, what the Thing was like, what the mosaic floor was like, and so on.

Mr. Burrows told them enthusiastically how marvelous the cave really was. He asked Roger and Stephen how they thought the pictures had kept so clear and undamaged. All Stephen could suggest was that the fluke of the bomb exploding farther up the woods had diverted the stream so that the water seeped down across the woodland space between the crater and the cave. There it dripped into the cave and kept the mosaic floor clean and bright. It seemed a miracle that there was just the right amount of wetness to clean but not to wear away the mosaics. Mr. Burrows also told about how he had been staggered at the tree root ceiling. In fact, he said, he had been so excited down there that he had nearly forgotten the big black rusty Thing in the corner.

Mrs. Gray asked if it was safe to leave the cave and its

dreadful occupant alone and unguarded overnight. The two men decided it was, but agreed that they would have to warn Jim the farmhand, and Alb 'Erratt when he came in the morning. In the morning too they would decide whom to telephone about disposing of the thing. No one could see any easy way to solve the big problem: how to dispose of the bomb without also disposing of the marvelous mosaics. No one said it, but it was at the back of everyone's mind that with a rusty old bomb like that there was not much chance of moving it away from the cave so that it could be dealt with or even exploded harmlessly somewhere else. There were no roads or even smooth patches of ground that would make moving the bomb possible.

It was a very gloomy Land Roverful that drove back to Burrows' Farm that evening, and they left behind them an anxious group at Grays' Farm. Mark's last words to Roger and Stephen as they went up to bed were, "Perhaps some'ut'll turn up in the morning. You never know. Keep your chins up. Perhaps . . ." He hadn't the heart to finish it when he saw Roger's miserable face.

"Steve," came a husky whisper in the darkness an hour later.

"What?"

"They can't just blow it up and ruin all the cave, can they?"

"I dunno, Rog. I just don't. I suppose someone'll have to decide what's most important—the risk of the bomb going off when anyone went near it, or those mosaics and what else there might be in the cave."

"It's been safe so long. Why can't they just . . . ? Oh, gosh, it's rotten. I can't . . ." His voice became muffled and Stephen guessed that his head was buried miserably in his pillow.

"Leave it till morning. Something might turn up. Someone'll have a bright idea."

But Stephen felt less hopeful than he sounded. What could anyone have a bright idea about? There were two certainties. The bomb had to be disposed of. As far as he knew, that meant blowing it up . . . if it didn't go off by itself in the middle of the night. From what Roger and Mark had said, it seemed they had done everything to the "Statue" short of starting a pneumatic drill on it. They quite likely had set the time fuse going, if it had one. It might not be just an unexploded ordinary bomb, but an unexploded time bomb. In any case, whether a bomb squad blew it up or it blew itself up, the wonderful Dragon's Cave was done for. There wasn't, as far as he could see, the remotest hope of moving the bomb and exploding it somewhere else. After rotting slowly for twenty years it must surely be too risky to move? What rotten luck. That Dragon and the Loch Ness Monster and the Scorpion were real art, thousands-of-years-old masterpieces, and now almost certain to be blown up. Poor old Roger, he thought finally. This is *not* one of his bits of luck after all—unless you count bad luck.

"Steve!" Wild hands pulling at his shoulder.
"Gerrout . . . Go 'way . . . Stop it!"
"Steve! Wake up. I've got it."
Roger! It was that menace Roger again. "Go away!

. . . What the pip!" He had pulled all the bedclothes off! He was shining a faint flashlight right in Stephen's eyes.

"I've got it. I've thought of a way to save the cave."

"What? Oh no, not again." Stephen looked at the window, still black. Not a glimmer of dawn. "Go to sleep. Talk about it in the morning . . . Stop shaking me, you rotter!"

"Listen then. Who cares about sleep! I tell you, I've thought of a way out."

Stephen groaned, rubbed his eyes, angrily pushed the staring yellow eye of the flashlight away, and sat up. "What are you yapping about? Honestly, Roger, you're a menace."

"The cave and the bomb. We must go and see Alb 'Erratt first thing in the morning, soon as it's light, and ask him if he can see to the bomb. He'll know what to do. That was his job in the war, wasn't it? He told me himself. He'll be able to make it safe."

Stephen snarled and dived back under the bedclothes. "You go and wake me in the middle of the night for that? You menace, you . . . Oh, shut up, can't you, and let's get some sleep? Just shut up and go back to bed. You'll wake the whole house up."

He heard Roger stumble away in the darkness and lie down, utterly still. When his irritation had cooled, he raised himself onto an elbow and whispered across the room. "Rog! I say, Rog."

"What?" Miserably.

"Sorry. I'm tired . . . It's not a bad idea. Maybe

Alb 'Erratt will be some help. We'll see, first thing tomorrow. O.K.?"

"Yes, O.K. Good night, Steve."

"Good night."

"Steve."

"*What?* Can't you go to sleep? Can't you wait till tomorrow . . . ?"

"That's it. You said first thing tomorrow . . . Today, you mean. It's getting light already."

Stephen blearily forced open his eyes and focused them agonizingly on where he guessed the window was. Soon he could detect a faint grayness where the blackness had been before.

"Yeah," he grunted, heavily, sighingly, wearily. "Yeah . . . today . . . first thing today." He fell instantly back into the depths of sleep. He had a full undisturbed twenty minutes before Roger, fully dressed and breathlessly eager, woke him and forced him to get up too.

Once they were moving, the sweet, cool air of the early June morning woke Stephen up deliciously and completely, like a swift plunge into a swimming pool he had known was going to be chilly. And in running he could get back at Roger, whose legs could not manage the pace Stephen set. Neither could Mark's, so Stephen, in decency once his exhilaration in the early daytime and the purity and the freshness of the fields and woodlands had calmed down, slowed his jog-trot to something they could equal without bursting a lung.

They had raced away from the farm so as to catch Alb 'Erratt before he was sent out or set on his day's work at Grays'. Mark said Alb started at about six with the milking, so they had to get there well before that. Mark had thought Roger's idea of asking Alb 'Erratt for help was a pretty hopeless idea, but he agreed it was the only remaining chance. Nothing had been said to Mark's parents, who were too busy to notice that the three boys were up and about.

The sleepy *coo-coo-coo, coo-roo* of wood pigeons high up in the oak tops of Middle Finger drifted down to them as they trotted along the wood's edge, keeping on the short-cropped turf by the side of the path, and as they turned with the path to face the wide top joint of Third Finger the clouds parted and the flaring sun poured its brilliance through the tree tops ahead and dazzled the six young eyes. A cuckoo swept down from the branches of the nearest tree and threw its jerking notes across the fields. The sweet, sickly perfume of the wild parsley by the woods' wire fence, the flickering sunlight shuttering through the closely ranked tree trunks, the drifts of yellow and blue where the nettles and bluebells showed, the calls of countless birds as the dawn chorus ended, the springy feel of the ground beneath their hurrying shoes, all combined to make the swiftly passing moments of this anxious little journey a tiny dream of heaven.

Stephen felt a warm happiness swell over him that he was there at the moment of time when the world was perfect. Such beauty all around him, and to think that he hadn't even begun one painting yet. Ah, well, first things first, and Roger's cave discovery and everything that followed from that certainly had become the first priority.

"Nearly there now." Mark's gasped words jolted Stephen back to the present and he saw that they were approaching the gap in the Third Finger woods where a tiny brick bridge carried a farm track over the brook. Fifty yards up the track on the other side of the little valley was the cluster of buildings around the Grays' Farm.

The three boys walked the last few yards, to have enough breath left for talking. Roger realized that he had about the most important bit of pleading ahead of him that he had ever had to do. Somehow he had no doubts about succeeding.

As they reached the farmhouse itself, Stephen saw a pink pajama-coat pressed against an upstairs window. Above it he could make out Jane's face and fair hair. She hurried to push the window open and call out in surprise, "What's up? Anything happened?"

"No, not yet. We're just going to try . . . Oh, you'd better come and help us. Come on. We'll be over by the milking sheds," Stephen said anxiously. Now they were here it suddenly seemed very unlikely that Alb 'Erratt would be the answer they had all hoped for.

Jane and a very sleepy Sarah, both with hair tousled and clothes thrown on any way, joined the three boys in a few seconds.

"What's *up?*" Sarah insisted. "It's only a quarter to six. Have you lot gone mad? What *is* going on?"

"We're going to see if Alb 'Erratt can suggest anything about the bomb," said Roger.

Sarah said, "Oh . . . But why? I don't see—"

"Shut up and wait then," growled Jane, for at that moment the white-overalled figure of Alb 'Erratt came around the corner. He stopped in surprise when he saw the five serious faces lined up before him.

" 'Ello," he said cheerily. "Come to do me milking for me?"

"No not really, Mr. 'Erratt," said Roger. "Can we have a word with you?"

"Sure. What about?"

"Have you seen Mr. Gray this morning yet?"

"No, but he'll be here any minute, I guess. We usually do the milking together. Why?"

"We want to ask a favor of you. A big favor, because you're the only one who can help us, and it's something terrifically important."

"Sounds mysterious. What's so special about me?" Alb was puzzled. All five faces were strained and solemn.

"Can you come with us for half an hour, so we can show you something, please?" said Roger.

"Half an hour! I'm supposed to be milking. I know I'm a bit early, but I haven't got half an hour to spare."

"Couldn't you possibly, Mr. Herratt?" said Jane. She felt someone must support old Roger, who had done all the pleading so far. "It's terribly urgent and you're the only one. . . ."

"I can't see why it's got to be me and why it's got to be now." Alb frowned. "Tell me what it's all about."

"We can't tell you. We've got to show you. You can't understand until you've seen it. No one could. Please. *Please*, Alb, come and see." Roger was white with anxiety. He didn't want to stand there arguing. He wanted to grab Alb's arm and hurry him down to the woods and the cave. If they stayed there much longer Mr. Gray might come and tell Alb everything and order them all not to go near the cave again.

"O.K. I give in." Alb was a man of quick action once he had decided a thing. He ran into the shed and called out to Jim that he'd got to go with the young'uns for a few minutes. Jim agreed to start the milking for him. Then Alb bustled out, no longer wearing his white overall, his brown face more wrinkled than ever with bewilderment as the five all grabbed him and hurried him down the lane and away.

They started walking, then began hurrying, and finished trotting. Alb did not mind. He was lean and wiry and could run as easily as dawdle. Only Sarah protested, but Jane mercilessly took her arm and forced her to keep up.

"It won't run away," Sarah managed to gasp out.

"Chump! We haven't got long. Mr. Gray'll miss him and come and stop us if we don't get there quickly." Jane was thankful she had been awake and looking out of the window when the boys arrived, otherwise they would never have been able to let her and Sarah join in.

Alb 'Erratt too began to protest when he saw how far he was being taken, but his worries were overcome. The five children would stop at nothing now. The last chance was going to be played out as far as humanly possible.

Into the woods they hurried, along the winding path, where startled blackbirds flew noisily up, their warning notes resounding among the trees, and once a big doe rabbit shot across the track, nearly tripping Roger up. At last, a few steps from the cave, they all gathered, panting and excited.

"Blimey, you are a sudden lot," puffed Alb. "Why stop here? It's only another fifty miles to the seaside. Let's keep on running. I feel like a paddle. We'll be there by next week if we don't stop."

"Sorry, Alb. It must seem queer, but you'll understand soon now." Roger looked at Stephen and said, "You coming with us, Steve? Or shall I show Alb by myself?"

"Let me go by myself with him," said Stephen. The feeling that the bomb really might go off at any moment had got inside him, and he hated the thought of going into the cave again. Yet he was the oldest and ought to, he reckoned.

"No, I'm going," said Roger definitely. So, telling Mark and the girls to stay right back, Stephen followed Alb 'Erratt, who himself followed Roger toward the holly bush.

When the three of them were safely down the two steps and standing firmly on the floor, Roger produced and lit the candle stubs he had been careful to remember. He also shone the flashlight around to show the cave's first tourist all the wonderful discoveries they had made. The little man was spellbound. As the boys had done the first time they had seen the mosaics, he seemed to gaze on every tiny square of stone separately before he was satisfied that he had seen it all. He delighted them by his gasping amazement and appreciation of the beauty of the designs and the colors and the living, moving appearance of the beasts at his feet. At last he found his voice.

"You again, young Roger, I dare bet. You found it, didn't you? What a rare chap you are. Fancy finding a place like this! Better'n a gold mine. What a treasure!"

Then he saw the root ceiling and was again flabbergasted at the new marvel. By the time he had been shown the coins, the bead, and the piece of ancient glass handle he was in a state of stunned bewilderment. All he could say again and again was: "What a lad you are. Don't just about everything happen to you? What a lad you are!"

His delight in the cave was so real and so spontaneous and so repeated that the two guides had little chance to think about the Thing which was leaning half in and half out of the shadows up in the far corner of the cave. Finally Roger thought that he must break the spell.

"It's so marvelous you wouldn't want it destroyed, would you, Alb?'"

"Destroyed? This? It'd be wicked. No one could let that happen. But . . ." He broke off. puzzled. "What's likely to happen, then? And what did you want me for down here? What was it that couldn't wait?"

"This is the trouble," said Stephen quietly. He took the flashlight from his brother and shone it on the Thing. It gleamed dully and evilly in the yellow light.

"That? What is it?"

"We reckon it must be an old bomb, one that the Germans— Why, Alb, what's wrong?" Roger broke off in alarm as the little man, with a hoarse cry of fear, jerked back and stared wildly around the dim cave at the two boys.

"A bomb! An' you brought me here to see this? Get out of 'ere, quick!"

He pulled them furiously toward the cave's mouth, and then, stumbling up the worn earth steps, he tumbled into the open air and ran some yards away from the cave. There he leaned haggardly against a birch tree's shining trunk until the boys came up to him.

"Alb, I'm sorry, I really am," Roger said miserably. "I didn't know you felt like that about them. I thought you might tell us what to do about it. We just didn't want all that cave blown up." His voice tailed off dejectedly. He seemed to have given up to despair.

Stephen explained further. "We didn't think it was all that dangerous. I reckon it's been there twenty years." He told Alb how his map, with the four holes plotted on it, had suggested the missing fifth hole and had led them all to suppose that the black metal cylinder in the cave was the missing bomb. He ended by saying "We couldn't think of anyone else who could help. You know about bombs, so Roger said, and we hoped you'd be able to suggest something, anything, so that the cave didn't get blown up."

"Is Mr. Herratt going to help?" Sarah and Jane and Mark had quietly joined them.

"Any idea yet?" said Jane.

"I don't think Mr. Herratt can do anything," said Stephen sadly.

"Then the cave's a goner," said Mark angrily. "Well, it 'adn't ought to be allowed. There ought to be some way o' getting that blasted bomb out o' there."

Roger, who was near to tears with disappointment, turned away from the others and began trudging back toward the path.

"Where are you going, Roger?" asked Stephen.

"Back to the farm. It's no use. It's all no use." With head hanging down and shoulders slumped, Roger looked like a cartoon figure of gloom.

Alb 'Erratt had thrown off his first spasm of fear. He was gray-faced and quiet, but he walked after Roger and pulled him back. The look of deep misery in the boy's face made him forget his own dread. He said, "Wait a minute, lad. Let's talk it over a bit longer. Perhaps I was a bit hasty." He grinned, but the grin seemed not quite real to Stephen, who looked at the little man with new hope. "When you been blown up and 'ad your head just about filled with bits of old iron from a Jerry bomb, well, you act a bit shy the next time." He added, to no one in particular and only just loud enough for the others to hear, "Twenty-year-old; might be safe by now. . . ."

He slapped Roger on the back. "O.K., lad. You've got me. I'll go and have another look. Only, you lot stay back. Right back. No need for more than one of us to become shredded meat. Go on, back."

He watched the delighted children step a few yards back, told them to lie down behind a fallen log and wait till he called. Then he strode confidently back to the cave and disappeared behind the holly bush and underneath the exposed root system of the birch tree.

The five onlookers held their breath. This was it, the moment of decision, the last chance of the last chance. Would Alb 'Erratt be able to save the Dragon's Cave?

17
The Fifth Hole

Five young bodies sprawled on their stomachs behind the lichened old log. Five seats of jeans turned upward to the glorious June sky. Five pairs of eyes anxiously peered toward the dark green holly leaves and the glistening white sloping birch trunk. Not all five minds were concentrating on the vital point, though.

Jane said, "What can he *do?*"

Stephen said, "Tell if it's a bomb or not."

"We know it is, don't we?"

"Not for hundred percent certain."

"Then what?" said Mark.

"Tell if it's safe," said Roger, "I suppose."

"Then what?"

"I dunno." Irritably: "You tell me."

"What about Mr. Gray?" Sarah's mind had strayed to other possibilities. "When he finds Alb isn't doing the milking, surely he'll come and see . . . ?"

"Let's hope he's too busy. Anyone got any grub? Must be breakfast time. I'm starving."

"Roger, how could you? Food *now*! My stomach's all tied up in knots, wondering what's going to happen."

"Well it's a jolly hungry sort of morning, and we ran miles before you were up."

"Here 'e is," said Mark excitedly. "'E's coming back, an 'e's grinning like a toothpaste ad."

They all stood up, hearts hammering, wondering what the white-haired little man was going to say.

"Well, Mr. 'Erratt?" said Roger, taut-faced and quiet.

"Alb! Alb! Not Mr. 'Erratt to me friends, I keep telling you." He was grinning widely. Stephen, however, noticed that his eyes were sharp and bright. His forehead had a faint gleam of sweat on it. Alb pulled out his red handkerchief—the same one Roger had had tied around his sprained ankle—and wiped his brow.

"Bit close in that cave," he said. "No proper ventilation. Couldn't find how the windows opened." He sat down astride the log they had lain by and casually said, "It's O.K., you young 'uns. Don't know what I was so scared for." He looked unconcernedly across the woodlands—or was it, Stephen wondered, watching him closely, just an act he was putting on? Alb went on. "Reckon it's safe enough now. Like you said, lad"—he spoke to

Stephen—"twenty years or more and the explosive inside goes all rotten. I should think it's no more dangerous than an empty oil drum now. I'll get it out o' that cave for you, don't worry."

"Oh, gosh, Alb, that's wonderful! That's great!" Roger was nearly dancing for joy. "Then the cave'll be safe. That's marvelous! Thanks, Alb. Thanks a million." He slapped his friend on the back in delighted relief. Alb quickly reminded them all: "Yes, well, glad to help, but I got my milking to do, remember?" They did. "Right, then. You all go on back to the farm and tell Mr. Gray this 'ere bomb needn't bother anyone. Leave it to me. You go back now, quick as you can, and catch him before he comes down here. Tell him I'm coming in a minute. And then stay up there and have your breakfasts. No need to come back. I'll be coming up there myself in a little while. Off you go. Shoo!"

Chattering with relief and delight the five youngsters made their way back along the path through the woods. Stephen hesitated just before going out of sight of the little figure standing by the fallen tree and even called back, "Sure you don't want me to stay and help, Mr. Herratt?" But he got a quick shout of, "No! You run off and do me milking. Go on—buzz off!" So he buzzed off and joined the other four. They were all saying what a fine chap Alb 'Erratt had turned out to be. Even Mark had forgotten his former prejudices and was admitting that the little man was "a proper good 'un."

"Saved our bacon, 'e 'as, I reckon," he said.

Jane licked her lips and said, "That's just what I want

now—with two fried eggs and some fried bread—luscious, sizzling, juicy bacon. Do you think your aunt'll give us some, Mark?"

They raced up the fields until their breath gave out, and then glowingly and happily walked back to breakfast.

The moment the five youngsters had gone from sight Alb 'Erratt's face changed. The cheerful grin he had forced himself to show faded away to leave a tight-lipped, narrow-eyed anxiety. The little man took a deep breath and then stepped back to the cave.

He let himself down into the semi-darkness and stared in horrified fascination at the sinister black shape leaning against the mud a few feet from him, the waning candle-light flickering as his arrival stirred up air currents in the cave. Alb gritted his teeth, thought of the joy on young Roger's face when he had said the bomb wasn't dangerous, and stepped toward the rusty canister.

A wave of horror and panic swept over him as he came within reach of it. Memories, a score of years old, of a London street near the docks, of a blinding flash and a great clap of thunder, of searing pains in his chest and head, of the awful pit of agony he had slipped down into, then the weeks and months of operations and lying in pain in hospital: all these poured into his mind at the sight of this wicked monster, lying in wait only inches away from him. He felt the sweat running off his forehead and trick-ling into his eyes. His mouth was dry and his lungs burned from the deep gulps of air he was making himself take. He forced his hands to go out and feel the thing.

How loose was it? Had the boys got it clear of the

mud? He gently exerted some strength and moved it up-right. Good. It seemed quite free. Stephen must have arrived with his warning just before Roger and Mark had had time to try to move it. Alb tested its weight. Just manageable. That would be about a hundred-pounder—or a German fifty-kilogram bomb. Small, but that's all the German bombers could carry early in the war. Anyway it was lucky. Anything bigger would have been too big to move without a lot of tackle. He moved a candle stub out of the way and put his arms firmly around the rusty metal.

Sweating so much that he feared his hands would be too slippery, he heaved the monster gently off its mud cradle. He could just lift it. He took a few staggering, careful steps across the glistening mosaic floor, reached the cave mouth, and let down the bomb to the bottom step. He bent down and put his ear to the cold metal. A few seconds while all he could hear was the blood pumping through his head were enough to satisfy him. He heaved the ugly thing up again, forced it up to his chest height with a final spurt of strength, and thankfully felt it resting on the top step. Just as he was feeling calmer with relief that all had gone so well so far, he found his hands shaking. He stared, horrified, at his fingers, wrists, and forearms as they twitched in a paroxysm of nervous fear. Angrily he clasped his hands together and forced them both to be still. When the attack was over he was wringing with sweat and weak as a helpless, newborn babe. It was several minutes before he felt strong enough to heave himself up to stand on the first step.

He stood balanced slightly forward, with the bomb in between his feet. Could he lift it up on to the woodland floor without slipping or overbalancing off the step? Were his hands too sweaty? Had he sufficient nerve to try?

After several rasping deep breaths he forced himself to bend. His back strained, his neck muscles bulged, his arms felt torn from their sockets, and his legs burned with fatigue as his scratched and bleeding hands grasped the rough metal cylinder and with the last remnants of his strength forced it up and out into the light of the June morning. Feverishly he scrambled up after it, and before his legs and arms and will once more failed him, he carried it like a delicate, sleeping baby, cuddled in his arms against his middle. Uncounted steps farther on he let it slip slowly and gently to the earth. It lay black and ugly on the grass and wild flowers, crushing a cluster of bluebell heads beneath its mud-smeared casing.

Twenty yards away, collapsed behind a safe tree trunk, Alb 'Erratt lay on the woodland floor too. He was gasping, sobbing, and shuddering with the release of fear and effort. At least the cave would be safe now. Those lads wouldn't need to worry about those marvelous pictures. They had been brave to mess around in the cave like that after they knew the Thing was a bomb. Stupidly, crazily, recklessly plucky. And Alb smiled as he imagined their delight when they knew the bomb had been removed.

He felt better already. That was enough rest. Another lift and carry now. Must get the thing out of the woods into the open where it could be dealt with. He wearily stood up and crept back to his waiting burden.

It took him three more stages before finally he stood in the open field, a good way up the slope, with the bomb many yards clear of the woods and clear of him. It was done. It could be blown up safely now. The Dragon's Cave was safe.

Alb sat down weakly on the grass and lay back. The sky had grown a few cotton clouds which were swimming swiftly across the clear blue. Strong wind up there. But down in the hollow it was warm and sheltered. The pigeons were cooing lullabies from the woods, the bees were swerving in and out of the buttercups all around him, and the sun was warm on his face. His eyes stared upward and he relaxed, at peace with himself, knowing he had overcome his great fear.

The sound of the Land Rover coming down the fields woke Alb from his daydreaming. He scrambled up and ran over to the track, waving the vehicle to a halt.

"Best not go any farther, Mr. Gray," he said.

"Alb, what the devil've you been up to?" demanded Mr. Gray, putting the hand brake on. He, Mr. Burrows, and Jim Stead the cowman all climbed out.

"Nothing much, boss. Sorry I'm missing a bit of the milking, but I've been lugging that ol' bomb out of the cave."

"You've what?" They stared disbelievingly at him.

"Aye, there it is, down there. See?" He pointed down the slope. "Rusty ol' thing. Cut my hands a bit, but it'll blow up nice and safe now. You going to ring up the police about it . . . or . . .?"

"Blow up, man? You told those youngsters it was safe. What do you mean, blow it up?" Mr. Burrows snorted.

"Ah well, I didn't want them to know. No need to let them go on worrying. But I reckon the Army blokes'll want to blow it up, to be safe. Won't do no harm, boss. Just dig a nice round hole in the field." Alb grinned.

"I don't know about you, Alb! You're as daft as those kids, messing about with an old bomb." Mr. Gray sounded bewildered.

Mr. Burrows said earnestly, "Damn plucky thing to

do, Alb. More than I'd like to do. And after you'd been blown up once. Damn plucky."

"And you've saved the cave. Those young 'uns'll be pleased. Alb, I'll shake your hand, man." And Mr. Gray did. The others did too. Then, leaving Jim on guard to see that no one went near the bomb, they drove Alb back to the farmhouse to have his scratched hands seen to and to spread the good news. The Ferns, Barrs, Burrows, and Grays could not say enough in praise of Alb's bravery. The little man grinned delightedly, and joined in the breakfast Mrs. Gray had been waiting to serve for the five hungry children. He sat next to Roger, whose eyes glowed with admiration and gratitude when he heard all that Alb had done and had risked.

"Thanks, Alb. Thanks a million. I knew you could do it. Thanks!" was said not once but dozens of times. The kitchen rang with the bellowed three cheers that Mark proposed for the white-haired hero. Mr. Burrows had to come to ask for a bit less noise so that he could phone Mark's mother and tell her everything.

From then on the telephone was in great demand. There were calls to the police, who said they would see about getting some Army experts to come to deal with the bomb. ("You're sure it's a bomb, Mr. Gray?" the police sergeant kept insisting.) Another call went to Mr. Fern at Cambridge, to tell him about the cave and the mosaics, and to ask him to get his friend at the University to come to see everything. Another call went to Bristol, where Mrs. Barr, like everyone else, had to be told many, many times before she believed the story.

Then, because it was still so early in the morning, there seemed a very long time to wait. Mr. Gray arranged for Alb to take over from Jim on guard duty after breakfast was done. Mrs. Burrows arrived and heard all the story in detail. A police car from the town drove up, and two constables were led down the fields to take over sentry duty from Jim instead of Alb. The inspector was very puzzled that any man would risk his life to carry a highly dangerous old bomb some hundreds of yards just to save some trees from being blown down. Everyone had agreed that none of the strangers—police, Army, or anybody else who came about the bomb—need be told the real reason for moving it.

The children helped around the farm, the boys in the yard and the girls with the housework and cooking. They all wanted to be near when the bomb was blown up, even though, as Roger pointed out, this was their last day, and there was a terrific lot of Left Hand Wood still to be explored.

At about midday a green-painted truck drove up and a young lieutenant got out. The children crowded around the truck while Mr. Gray and Alb explained about the bomb. Inside the truck were four men, some big boxes and reels of wire and lots of small sacks. Alb was invited into the cab of the truck to show the soldiers the way. The children ran ahead to open the field gates.

By one o'clock the bomb-disposal squad had piled sandbags all around the old bomb and had begun wiring up the detonation charge. Mr. Gray came then to pass on to everyone the invitation to dinner at the farmhouse, so the children piled into the now nearly empty truck, and with the soldiers and one policeman, were bumped and bounced back to dinner. The policeman hurried over his food and then left to take his friend's place while he came back for his meal.

Finally, at a quarter to four the lieutenant walked back up the grassy slope to the circle of onlookers. "Everything go-go, as the Americans say," he said. "Permission to blow a hole in your field, Mr. Gray?"

"Sure, go ahead and blow the dratted thing up." Mr. Gray chuckled.

"O.K., sergeant. Let her go."

As all eyes, fascinated, watched the little brown mound in the distance the sergeant pressed the plunger home. The click of the metals meeting in the switch box was followed a split second later by a dull thud from down the field. The piled-up sandbags showered in a thousand tatters upward. Earth and stones fell dully down, dust and grayish smoke hovered a few moments and then drifted lazily away along the woods' edge.

"O.K.," said the young lieutenant. "Another old Jerry bang-bang done for. Want to have a look, you young 'uns?"

When they reached the freshly torn soil and saw the size of the hole, the children all became very quiet. Roger was the first one to say what everyone was thinking. "Gosh, it's as big a hole as the others. And we poked that old bomb and bashed it and . . ." Words failed him.

Stephen said, "Yes, and Alb 'Erratt carried it all the way up here. I reckon he knew, too. It hadn't rotted away. It was as dangerous as ever."

Mark said, "Cor! He's a proper good 'un, en't 'e?"

Jane said softly, "Just imagine if it had gone off in the cave!"

Sarah said, "If I'd known the bomb was as strong as this, I'd jolly well have shouted ten times as loud when we gave Alb three cheers this morning."

The soldiers and the policemen, walking back to the truck, were amused a few seconds later to hear five lusty young voices bawling once more a heartfelt, "Hip, hip, hooray—hip, hip *hooray*—*hip, hip,* HOORAY!" Mr. Gray and Mr. Burrows knew what it was all about and slapped the grinning Alb on the back again and again.

As soon as he was back at the farm, Stephen got out his sketch map and penciled in a new item, the fifth hole.

Next day—Saturday afternoon—a picnic party took place in the woods by the Dragon's Cave. It was a huge one. There were seven Barrs, five Ferns, three Burrows, two Grays, one Herratt, and one new face.

The new face was an excited one. Dr. Hopper from Cambridge had driven down in record time to inspect the cave and had pronounced it the discovery of the decade. Alb 'Erratt, a handy man with a saw as well as with a bomb, had constructed some wooden steps to make entry into the cave easier for anyone who did not want to have to squirm in on their stomach, for the two earth steps had by now become so worn that they were no longer usable. Mr. Gray had fixed up an electric inspection lamp that worked from a big car battery, and everyone had been shown around the marvels of the floor of the old Roman villa. The four other children, the three younger ones from Bristol, Mary, Peter, and Anne, and Tim Fern had especially been thrilled. Tim had not wanted to come up the steps again. He had wanted them to fetch a camp bed so that he could stay to guard Roger's cave. He had heard someone talking about what treasures the mosaics were and thought someone might steal the cave. But the grown-ups were just as staggered at what their children had been up to, and all still wore the dazed look that people have when something impossible happens before their eyes. Roger had shown everybody the gaping, raw wound in the field which they now called the Fifth Hole, and there were not a few gasps when Alb 'Erratt's part in saving the cave was again explained.

The picnic was a jolly one. The early summer's day was perfect, Left Hand Wood looked its best—even though the bluebells were fading fast—and a great new treasure had been discovered and saved after sixteen hundred years. There was the thrill of expectancy in the minds of all those big enough to understand, for who knew what other treasures lay hidden under the woodland soil? Even the children's fears about Left Hand Wood being spoiled and turned into a tourist center had been dispelled by Dr. Hopper. He had asked and obtained permission from Mr. Gray and Mr. Burrows to bring a full team of experts down in a day or two's time to do some test diggings in the woods near the cave, and to sift the cave's soil still further, and especially to safeguard the mosaic floor. He said the mosaic pictures were amazing, and was excited by their fine state of preservation. He was horrified when the boys described their methods of excavation and searching, and said they had better join his next dig and learn how to take care of every crumb of soil near such priceless discoveries. He was surprised at Roger's Nero coin— "Brass, not gold, young man. Nothing like gold really. But it's an unusually early coin to be found in Britain. Hope we find some more. Lovely bead, that is. Beautiful."

He had measured, photographed, and pegged out the woodland ground all around the cave, and had rubbed his hands in glee at the thought of the dig he was going to do there. He quite agreed with Roger and the others that the woods were too lovely to spoil, even for a fine new Roman mosaic discovery, and had promised to damage nothing.

Stephen asked whether the cave couldn't be kept as a cave, like the ones at Lascaux in France, where the wall paintings were scientifically protected against wear and weather damage. Dr. Hopper said he did not know, but he would do all he could to find the best way of keeping the marvels of both woods and cave unspoiled.

"Listen, everybody," Dr. Hopper called at last when the picnic was well underway. "Listen. I propose we drink a toast. Has everyone got a glass or cup of something? Good. Now, first I think we should toast young Roger Fern here, for discovering this cave and all its treasures. Then, too, Stephen Fern, who had the wit to work out that complicated business of the holes and the unexploded bomb being the statue and so on. And last, a very brave chap, who saved it all from destruction—Alb Herratt. Now, everybody, raise your glasses of pop and your teacups to these three—Roger, Stephen, and Alb Herratt."

"Roger! Stephen! Alb Herratt!" shouted everyone, and

moments later the farthest corners of Left Hand Wood rang with the cheers that Jane started. "Hip, hip, hooray —hip, hip, hooray—*hip, hip,* HOORAY!"

"Mum, Dad," said Mark later that evening, when they were alone back at the farm. "I been invited to stay with Roger and Stephen in the August 'olidays. After that, can they come down 'ere again for a bit?"

"Hey, not so fast." Mr. Burrows chuckled. "Have that young Roger here again? Caves and Roman villas and bombs all in one short stay—and you want to have him here again? I'd better check my insurances and see if we're covered for earthquakes, avalanches, typhoons, and volcanoes erupting. Then we might let him come, eh, Molly?"

"Oh, Dad," said Mark, "I know everything 'appens to him, but it en't 'is fault. 'E's just an interesting chap to know."

"Son, you can say that again!" agreed Mr. Burrows.

"Mum, Dad," said Roger on the drive back to Cambridge. "I've changed my mind. I don't want to be a BBC recording engineer. I'm going to be an archaeologist."

"Good idea," said Mr. Fern.

"So," said Roger simply, "you won't mind asking old Birdie at school if I can have a few weeks off to go down to the cave and help Dr. Hopper with the dig, will you? I mean, if that's going to be my career now, I'd better get some practice, hadn't I? And it's my cave. So you will ask, won't you, Dad? Won't you?"

"Can I go too, Daddy?" said Tim, adding after a second or two, "If Mummy will come and do the cooking."

Nearly a week later, when the day's work had finished, Mr. Gray called Alb 'Erratt into the farmhouse. "Got something to show you, Alb," he said.

On the kitchen table stood a big cardboard carton.

"Present for you, Alb," said Mrs. Gray.

"For me, missus?" Alb was thoroughly surprised.

"Yes. The Burrows and us and Mr. and Mrs. Fern and the Barrs, and that Doctor of History from Cambridge, all thought you should have a little something as a thank you from all of us for what you did," said Mr. Gray.

"Oh, but . . ."

"So we puzzled a bit, and then young Roger told us what you wanted. So here it is. Have a look—then I'll run you down to your place in the Land Rover."

Alb, suddenly shy and embarrassed again, but very excited, began cutting string and pulling off brown paper. He gasped with pleasure when he saw what the package contained.

"It's a telly! Yes, I told young Roger I missed it after the hospital! Oh . . ." His face fell. "But I got no electricity in that little cabin o' mine."

"Doesn't matter, Alb." Mr. Gray smiled. "Look, this is a portable. Runs on these little batteries. It'll work anywhere. Just pull out this aerial and you're goggling. What about that, eh? Wonders of modern science!"

Dazed, but grinning delightedly, Alb carried his precious parcel to the Land Rover. He would not hear of it being jolted about on the floor, but nursed it all the way, hugging it fiercely as they bumped down the old, rarely used track that led to the disused stone quarries near his cabin.

"Thanks, boss," he said as he lowered the box onto his table. "Thanks to you all." His eyes twinkled. "Cor, started something that day, meeting young Roger, didn't it?"

"You're right, Alb. Things seem to happen around him. Now you'll want to switch on and try out your new toy, so I'll be off. Oh—" He paused in the doorway. "Here's the cash for the television license. I expect you'll have your money's worth. No, don't thank us anymore. You've earned it, man. You've earned it. Good night, Alb."

Mr. Gray stepped outside and walked slowly back to the Land Rover. Lovely old woods, these were. Delicious smell these pine trees had. He wondered how things were going at the diggings at the Dragon's Cave. Might stroll down after tea and see if he could help. Left Hand Wood —good name. Fitted the place. Always been beautiful, now it was more exciting than ever.

A thrush in one of the pines sent its notes clarinetting to the sky. Mr. Gray drove off very quietly in order not to spoil its song.